AROUND
THE
DARK DIAL

J.D. SANDERSON

Second Edition – Copyright © 2020

All rights reserved. No part of this publication may be reproduced, distributed, or transmitted in any form or by any means, including photocopying, recording, or other electronic or mechanical methods, without the prior written permission of the publisher, except in the case of brief quotations embodied in critical reviews and certain other noncommercial uses permitted by copyright law.

This is a work of fiction. Any characters, names, places, or likenesses are purely fictional. Resemblances to any of the items listed above are merely coincidental.

Cover design, interior design, and editing
by B.K. Bass.

Additional editing by Sam Hendricks and
Crystal L. Kirkham

For Charlotte.

ALSO BY J.D. SANDERSON

A Footstep Echo

The Clock's Knell

Table of Contents

Foreword	i
Hello There	1
Caller Four	17
The Simulant	39
Headline	59
Daughter	77
Hello Again	103
The Snowstorm	121
The Circus Peanut Gallery	139
Rearing	165
Choice	197
Welcome	211

FOREWORD

I remember thirty years ago, sitting on the couch with my father watching reruns of *The Twilight Zone*, *The Outer Limits*, and *Star Trek* (the original series). Each episode was its own, self-contained story. Each time we tuned in, we were presented with new ideas to fathom, new problems to solve, and new worlds to explore.

They say that television isn't like it used to be. For better *and* worse, this is true. Every generation has likely said this, but in the twenty-first century we're seeing a paradigm shift that is more dramatic than the differences between the likes of *Leave it to Beaver* and *Family Ties*.

Television in the 1950s and 60s was heavily influenced by radio dramas of the 1940s and 50s. The focus was on short narratives that could be consumed in a single sitting. You might have been welcomed back each week by familiar faces, but the problems they faced and the themes they explored would change from episode to episode. This trend continued through the 1970s and 80s, as well.

But, in the 1980s we began to see overarching

storylines independent of each episode's plot. The ongoing "will they or won't they" romance between Sam and Diane in *Cheers* is a prominent example of this.

Fast forward to today — in the age of streaming television and binge-watching — and we're seeing single stories play out over dozens of hours in shows like *The Walking Dead* and *Game of Thrones*. Each episode ends in a cliffhanger, and to get the whole experience you must watch every episode in order; waiting months or even years to find out how it ends.

You may have noticed I said television has changed for better *and* worse; not or.

I enjoy stories told in a *serial format*, where a single story is told over time in installments. I also miss the days of the *episodic format*, where single stories were told each time under a unifying framework of cast, setting, or theme.

Also, I think it behooves us to look back on the storytelling of days gone by; both to better understand where we are today, and to inspire us to tell our own stories in different ways. Should we ignore the storytellers of our fathers and grandfathers, we risk living in an echo chamber where all our stories follow a restrictive framework that quells any hope of innovation. Yes, the shift from episodic to serialized storytelling is a form of progress, but progress should not be embraced at the expense of tradition. Tradition, conversely, should not be embraced at the expense of progress.

I feel J.D. Sanderson understands this, and in

Around the Dark Dial he has embraced both tradition and progress. He is looking back at what came before, while keeping his eyes on the horizon and asking the eternal question: *What is next?*

While J.D. has embraced episodic storytelling in this collection, you may find some serialized storytelling waiting to surprise you. He has drawn inspiration from the golden era of science fiction, but he delves into modern-day concerns through that lens. He has looked back so that he might better help us look forward.

The stories collected in this volume share themes familiar to any fan of those old radio dramas and science fiction television of the 1950s and 60s. Each has an independent feel and a singular story to tell; but they all share themes of secrets, discovery, and — most importantly — humanity.

—B.K. Bass, Editor

AROUND THE DARK DIAL

HELLO THERE

"What do you say, Gerren? You ready to call it a morning?"

"I could stay out here all morning, Major."

Major Patel smiled as images from the survey engineer's helmet cam flooded her scopes. She looked up to the primary viewer at the front of the bridge where the main live feed had streamed for the past three hours. It was a safe assumption that half the world had tuned in by now to watch her survey team leader, Gerren Weber, walk inside the restricted space known as the field.

For the first time since the caldera erupted in 2024, a century ago, humans were entering what used to be Yellowstone National Park. The eruption could have wiped out most life across North America. It should have. But then the field appeared and contained the blast.

"I still can't believe how beautiful it is in here," Gerren mused aloud. His helmet cam showed him stepping over what had once been hardened lava. Lichen had long ago broken it down into a more suitable dwelling for plant life, which from their estimates had begun growing a year or two after temperatures had sufficiently cooled. "So much new life."

"There would appear to be dozens of new or mutated species seen on your feed alone," Patel replied with a smile. "Listen, Gerren, I think we've made great progress for the first survey. The rest of your team just made their way outside the field barrier. I'm satisfied if you are, and I know our crew back here are eager for a closer look at your data."

For a hundred years, the translucent green dome had resisted every scan and probe scientists could think of. And now her team had walked through it and were the first to see what secrets it was hiding.

"I don't suppose I could ask for a few more minutes, Major?"

Nodding, Patel replied, "A few more minutes, Gerren." She sipped her tea before turning back to her mic. "Let me guess. You're not staying to take a few extra soil samples, are you?"

"Guilty as charged, ma'am."

Patel rolled her eyes with a smile as the command crew let out a few snickers. Two days ago, she had received a call that a small child had fallen through the field after playing next to it with her dog. She had reemerged a few minutes later carrying a violet and white flower that botanists were not able to classify.

The ensuing media firestorm sent society careening off a proverbial cliff. Reporters and onlookers that had flocked from across the planet were denied access. Fearing a public health crisis or radioactive contamination, the president had ordered the military to surround the field and prevent anyone else from entering. Those attempting to rush the barrier were tackled and arrested.

Major Patel reported to Washington six hours after getting the call to meet her new team; an eclectic mix of civilian and military scientists. Gerren was the only face she knew. They had worked together on the second manned Mars polar survey a decade earlier. Like all brilliant scientists, he came with his own set of peculiar quirks.

"Genevieve?" she asked.

"You know me, Major," Gerren replied. Another ripple of laughter spread across the command crew as Gerren's helmet cam showed him pulling an antique film camera out of his pack.

"For God's sake, Gerren," Patel muttered as the viewer feed showed Gerren holding up his antique camera and snapping a picture. "Where do you even find film for something like that these days?"

"I want to know why he gave it that name," Lieutenant Okafor pondered.

"I got it from a little old lady in Rochester. Her grandmother had left her a ton of photographic relics. It took some doing, but I convinced her to sell me a few rolls." Gerren turned and snapped another picture. "And the name is old and classy, just like my camera."

"You do know your helmet cam takes better quality images than that thing ever could, right?"

"Maybe so, but this is so much cooler!"

"Five more minutes, Gerren, then I want you to head back," Patel said with a shake of her head. She turned back to her chair's controls to analyze the data streams from the helmet cam and suit sensors. The temperature, humidity, and pressure were all perfect for early spring. Everything looked exactly as it should be. While they had yet to document any animal life living inside the field, the flora sure put on one hell of a colorful show. Flowers, shrubs, and trees had been repopulating the landscape for years. Cut off from any form of human interference or development, it had become a beautifully overgrown display of Mother Nature.

"Major, the White House is requesting an update," Okafor reported.

"So much for having a few minutes to take in the view," Patel said. She reached for her headset and placed it over her head, centering the eyepiece.

"Major!" another young ensign called out. Patel stopped before activating her headset and looked at the primary monitor.

"What is it?" she asked.

"It's Gerren, ma'am. His heart rate just shot way up," the ensign replied.

"Okafor tell the president to stand by," Major Patel ordered.

"Captain?" Okafor asked.

"Gerren, what's going on?" Patel asked as she waved off the young lieutenant. "Gerren?"

Gerren's helmet cam was motionless. Ahead of him was a small break in the beautiful blue and green trees.

"Boost the audio," Patel ordered. "Vitals?"

"His heart rate is still spiking," Okafor replied. "Blood pressure and perspiration are also shooting up. I think something's spooked him, ma'am."

"Gerren, please respond," Patel requested before turning to a young officer in the back of the room. "Cut the feed to everyone but this room. We don't need half the planet going into a panic if something's happening." The boosted audio signal from inside Gerren's helmet filled the command center. His breathing was deep and heavy. Patel's brow furrowed as she listened.

"Can he hear us?" She asked.

"Yes, ma'am. Audio is transmitting, and there's no sign of interference," Okafor replied.

"Gerren, this is Major Patel. Please respond."

The helmet cam showed no movement. Gerren seemed fixated on that same area of woods. Patel stood up and walked over to the front of the command center, stopping a few feet from the primary monitor.

"What the hell are you looking at, Gerren?" Patel turned back to her command officers. "Somebody better get me some answers!"

The crew scrambled to see if they could get more data from the sensors on Gerren's suit and equipment. A minute later, a young ensign cried out as she pointed to the screen.

"Look!" she yelled.

The crew looked to see Gerren's hands slowly raise his antique camera up to his helmet. His gloved index finger pushed down on the shutter. He tracked a few centimeters to the right and snapped another picture.

"His heart rate is slowing," the young ensign relayed.

His camera tracked a few centimeters to the right. Patel and the crew watched as he snapped another few images. His gloved hand came up and adjusted the long lens before he stepped to the right. Gerren's finger was hitting the shutter faster than before. Patel lost count of how many pictures he had taken.

"What in blazes is he doing?" Patel whispered. "Gerren? Come in, please." The major waited another minute as Gerren took a step forward and snapped two more images.

The crew sat on the edge of their seats as Gerren's helmet camera snapped upwards. His index finger snapped the shutter a few more times as he panned up

and to the left. The camera stayed focused on the bright blue sky. Then, Gerren muttered something.
"Hello there."

*   *   *

Applause burst out from the onlooking crowd as Gerren emerged from the tree line. It continued as he made his way to the edge of the diminishing field. He gave a polite wave and smile to the mix of media, government officials, military, and civilians as he stepped through the faded screen.

Major Patel walked up to him and assisted with the removal of his helmet. She smiled as they both turned to wave to the crowd.

"Keep smiling," she glowered under her breath.

"I'm sorry, Major."

"Let's just get you inside. We're not going to have this conversation in front of the whole damned planet."

They acknowledge the crowd once again as they made their way back to the ramp of the main compound. Patel could hear a reporter talking about the mission being a rousing success despite a few technical difficulties with the feed. She breathed a small sigh of relief as the door closed behind them.

"Gerren, what the fuck happened out there?" Patel tried her best to keep her voice low.

"I am sorry, Major. It's just when I saw it..." Gerren paused as a pair of civilian contractors walked by them. "Did you cut the feed?" He set his camera down on a small table next to them.

"I did. You scared the hell out of us!"

"I know, but it scared the hell out of me."

"What did?"

"It! That thing. It was ten meters in front of me, for God's sake. Came out of nowhere." Gerren paused as Patel stared at him like he was crazy. "Didn't you see it?"

"Your helmet feed was active the entire time. We saw you looking at a small cluster of trees, and then the sky."

"You didn't... you didn't see it?" Gerren asked. His face turned pale. "But it was—"

"What?" Patel folded her arms as she looked up at the stammering survey engineer.

"It was right there! It looked at me. It was tall. Came out from behind the trees and stared at me. Then the damn thing just took off!" Gerren managed to keep his voice low as he flailed his arms around.

"We didn't see anything," Patel replied.

"But, you said you cut the feed."

"I ordered the feed cut because I didn't want half the planet to see you having a panic attack. I cut the feed because you scared us so badly that I didn't know what to say when the president called in asking for an update."

Gerren took a step back and leaned against the corridor wall. Patel stood next to him and put her hand on his shoulder.

"Gerren, let's get you down to the infirmary. The

stress of being the first person inside the field in over a century..."

"C'mon, Prisha! I'm not cranking up."

"Your vitals were through the roof."

"It was close to two meters high. Gray skin... or scales, I couldn't tell. Five limbs, two on top, three on the ground. It had black eyes!" Gerren started to raise his voice. "It made shapes, gestures with what I think was a hand. I snapped pictures of as many of them as I could; used up my entire roll. I think it was trying to tell me something."

"All right. Let's go," Patel ordered as she grabbed his arm and hurried him through the corridor. She stuffed him out of sight into a small meeting room near one of the analytics labs.

"Sit here, relax, and cool off." Major Patel pointed to a small couch next to a coffee table.

"I'm not cracking up," Gerren replied. "I saw something in the field. We need to find out what it is. Maybe it could explain how the field got there in the first place." His voice continued to rise as he spoke. "That's why we went in there, isn't it?"

"So your suit, jam-packed with the most expensive and advanced surveillance and recording equipment on the planet, just happened to miss whatever this thing was?"

"Yes!"

"It's not that I don't believe you, Gerren," Patel said with a sigh. "But try and see it from my point of view. No one can corroborate your story. No one in the command center saw anything on the monitor or in the sensor readouts."

"No one's been in there for a century! Hell, we couldn't even get a good look inside until it began to fade six months ago. How do we know what is and isn't ordinary in the field?" Gerren put his head into his hands and closed his eyes. He let out a long sigh before looking up at his commanding officer again.

"What are you going to do with me?"

"There will be an official debriefing," she replied. "You'll explain how the trip went as we review the data from your helmet cam and suit sensors, as well as any notes you inscribed into your pad. You should be on your way home with a nice paycheck by the end of the week."

Gerren looked up at her. "You're not going to hold me?"

"No," Patel said, "but I do want you to head over to the infirmary and see a doctor before and after you head home." She sat down next to him on the couch, placing her hand on his shoulder.

"Gerren, going in there like you did was incredibly brave. It's easy to get lost during a tough mission. It happens to the best of us. You gave us our first look into a part of the world cut off for generations. You should be proud of that. I'm proud of you."

"And you think I sound crazy."

"I don't think you're crazy. I think it's been a stressful few days of preparation and exploration. But you're going to be fine. You're still a hero to the entire world, you know," Patel said. "There's still years of research ahead of us as we try to learn what the field is, where it came from, and why it waited until now to dissipate. The data you collected is going to guide those top researchers. We all owe you, Gerren."

The survey engineer nodded his head before lowering it once again into his hands. He let out another deep breath as the adrenaline began to subside.

"Thank you, Major."

*   *   *

Gerren Weber turned on the viewing wall in time for the evening news brief. Information from team two was pouring out. They had spent twenty-four hours in the field, bringing back plant, soil, and insect samples.

He shook his head as images of the new six-person team flooded his wall. Major Patel was there to greet them, as was the President and several leading members of the scientific community.

Beneath the main viewer on the wall was the letter the President sent to everyone involved with his initial survey of the field interior. Gerren had not bothered to open it.

Gerren turned after hearing a knock at his front door. He walked over and opened it, smiling politely at the young woman holding a neatly wrapped package.

"Mr. Weber?"

"That's me," he answered.

"Scan here, sir," she instructed, holding out a small

pad. He pressed his thumb into the pad until the scanner gave off three soft beeps, then she handed the package over. Nodding to the delivery girl, he turned and closed the door behind him.

Gerren walked over to his kitchen table and set the box down. He used his thumbnail to slice open the sealer and removed a layer of packing paper from inside. He chuckled to himself as he saw his antique camera.

"Genevieve! I forgot all about you, didn't I?" he said to the camera as he picked it up.

The survey engineer, now at home for a 'well-earned extended rest,' as Major Patel had put it, walked over to the makeshift darkroom he had built a few years ago. He passed by his wall calendar. The following Monday was blinking blue, indicating another appointment with the shrink that Patel had suggested for him. The psychologist had diagnosed him as having suffered a sort of nervous breakdown due to work-related stress.

Gerren shut the door and turned on the soft, red light. He opened the back of the camera to discover the film he purchased weeks ago from the little old lady in Rochester was missing.

"Son of a bitch." He darted out the room, making his way back to the box still sitting on his kitchen table.

He pulled out another few layers of packing paper to uncover two small envelopes, the first of which had his name written on it. He opened the envelope and pulled out a small card.

Took the liberty of developing this for you. Stay put. We'll talk tomorrow.
   —Prisha

Gerren tossed the card aside and picked up the second envelope, pulling out nearly two dozen developed pictures. He could not help but admire the work — whoever did it knew their way around the old developing process.

The scientist smiled as he flipped through the first few photographs. He had snapped some beautiful shots of the field, the trees, and other new growth on the ground. Seeing them again brought back the exhilaration that coursed through his veins as he walked across the untouched landscape.

Gerren let out a long, fearful breath as he got to the eighth picture.

Two of its three legs were peeking out from behind one of those big, sturdy pines. The next picture revealed more. It could not have been any more than two meters in height, with a small mass in front of the chest that resembled a head. There was no identifiable mouth or nose. The only thing he could make out were two small, dark patches that could have been eyes.

He had reviewed the footage a dozen times with his psychologist. There had been nothing there. The footage collected by the rest of his team had shown nothing. In addition to the cameras on his helmet and array of sensors embedded in the suit, there was a constant stream of digital overlays and readouts inside the glass of each helmet. Gerren had turned off his digital display before grabbing his camera so he could focus on the scenery, leaving only a thin layer of glass between him and whatever this thing was.

The only thing besides his own eyes that had seen the strange creature was one of the most primitive types of image recording available.

"They couldn't see it," Gerren whispered. "They couldn't see it digitally."

Even from the detachment of a photograph, he could feel the intensity of its stare. There was no immediate sense of malice or anger. The closest thing he could think of was the feeling he got looking into the eye of a whale or dolphin. The intelligence was obvious, even if it was alien and unknown.

The graceful walk came back to him as he flipped through the thirteenth and fourteenth pictures. It had been unlike any kind of gait he had ever seen in a living creature. As he flipped the pictures, he could see the hand gestures he had described to his old friend.

It was hard to be sure, but he counted a total of nine fingers with webbing in between. They had moved around like a spider's web on the wind. There was a black opening in the middle of the palm. He had managed to get nearly twenty pictures of it gesturing with the alien hand.

The final two pictures showed the entity lifting off the ground. On either side of its hips, if that is what they were, were little appendages with openings. Gerren assumed that it used a form of organic propulsion to hurl itself dozens of meters in the air above his head. He managed to get one last blurry image of it in the air before losing it in the sunlight.

Gerren sat down on the couch as a tear streaked down his face. A small smile and laugh crossed his lips as his shoulders sank in exhaustion. His head bowed as the realization he hadn't imagined it after all rattled his core.

After collecting himself, Gerren turned back to one of the pictures of the gesturing hand. They were not random movements, but purposeful. His own hand lowered as he turned and looked over to a picture he had taken of his parents a few years ago, on their fortieth wedding anniversary.

They were smiling at each other as they held their hands out towards the camera. His mother was making the sign for the number four, while his father made the sign for zero. They had pressed their hands together to make the number forty. Gerren's mother was born deaf and had taught his father how to sign during their courtship.

He turned back to the picture of the tall, strange lifeform.

"Oh, God..."

Flipping through the photographs, he saw the tall organism move its webbed fingers from one image to the next. Three fingers were bent in one picture, then raised in another. Two others would touch another on the opposite side, then they would release.

A low, yet elated laugh left Gerren's mouth as he

leaned back into the soft, comforting caress of his couch. The heaviness of his eyelids grew as weeks of suppressed tension left his neck and shoulders. After a moment, he sat back up to stare down at the lifeform in the picture.

"What are you trying to say?"

CALLER FOUR

"We're going to go now to the east side of the city. Dan, you're on the Late Night Storey! What do you have for us?"

"Okay, so," the nervous caller began, "I saw something weird outside of my window last night. I mean, it was really weird, Terrance."

"Can you be a bit more specific?" Terrance Storey leaned forward as he reached up to adjust the well-worn microphone in front of his mouth. His board operator, Taye, gave him the signal that there was a hard break coming up at the bottom of the hour. He turned to look at the clock before nodding back.

"Well, it was like a group of lights. There's this really big tree outside my window, see? I got the house from my parents when they died. I never got around to cutting it down." Terrance rolled his eyes as he felt the caller start to meander.

"I get the picture, Dan. What were the lights doing?" Terrance asked.

"It was weird. They looked far away at first, then they seemed really close. Brighter, ya know? They seemed to come through the tree branches, not around them. It's a really big tree," the caller explained. "Then I realized they weren't lights at all."

"What were they?" Terrance asked.

"They were spirits," the caller continued." I felt this calming presence come over me. I think they were people I used to know. I've been hoping to see my brother again. He passed away last year."

"Have you had any encounters with spirits or other paranormal phenomenon before?"

"Yeah. When I was fifteen, there was this thing that came into my window at night. Scared the living hell out of me!"

Terrance muted his mic before taking a sip of his coffee. He listened as the caller rambled on about his ghostly experiences, occasionally shooting a look of curiosity to Taye. The host found it difficult to stifle a laugh as his shows' co-pilot held up a sticky note with the word "bullshit" written in black marker.

"Thank you very much, Dan. We've got a hard break here, but we'll be back at the top of the hour with more of your calls! If you've had a paranormal experience or otherworldly encounter, we want to hear about it on Late Night Storey!"

Terrance took off his headphones as the commercials and news break kicked in. He stood up to make his way out of the main studio.

"Didn't believe that last one, huh?" He asked Taye.

"Not one freaking bit," Taye replied. "He had all the credibility of a blind bank robbery witness."

Taye would have continued with his usual string of off-color humor had it not been for a few of the phone indicators lighting up. He nodded and answered the first one as Terrance shook his head and made his way over to the vending machines.

He had just celebrated the fifth anniversary of his program, which was now being heard in three cities across upstate New York. They had been on a bit of a dry spell booking guests, which meant that the callers had to carry the entire three hours of the show. Some nights brought fantastic stories. Others were like tonight.

Terrance reached down to grab a soda from the vending machine. The frantic waving of Taye's arm caught his attention as he came back up with his drink. The host trotted over to his faithful number two to see what was up.

"Why does that grin of yours always make me nervous?" Terrance asked.

"Got a good one for you. Caller four," Taye replied.

"Oh?"

"Yeah. Alien encounter I think."

"Nice!" Terrance exclaimed. He sat down at his chair, pulled his headphones on, and pulled the microphone closer. He nodded as the light came back on and cleared his throat.

"And we're back with Late Night Storey at 1:05 on a Wednesday morning! Thanks for staying with us. We're gonna jump right back into it with what I'm told is a possible extra-terrestrial encounter of some kind. Caller number four, Stacey, you're on with Late Night Storey!"

There was a small pause as they waited for the caller to speak. The line was active — Terrance could hear the faint hiss of the background air against the caller's phone.

"Stacey?"

"Hello?" A thin, wispy voice answered.

"Hello, you're on the air!"

"Sorry, I'm here. I had to close my door."

"That's okay. What do you have for the show?" Terrance leaned back from his microphone to take a sip from his drink.

"Something happened to me the other night," Stacey began. "I was getting ready to lay down, ya know, brushing my teeth and stuff. It all started after I got into bed."

"Can you describe the encounter?" Terrance leaned forward to place his elbow on the desk.

"Yeah," Stacey began. "I think I was asleep for a few minutes maybe, then I woke up."

"Anything in particular wake you up?"
"My dog was crying."
Shooting Taye a look of intrigue, Terrance asked, "Crying? As in whimpering?"
"Yeah," Stacey said. "I'm crate training him at night. He started whimpering from across the room in his crate."
"Incredibly common," Terrance mused. "Dogs have often shown the ability to sense a wide range of paranormal occurrences."
"He's a rescue, so at first, like, I just thought he was being a scared puppy. Then when I opened my eyes, I realized I couldn't get out of my bed."
Terrance could hear the woman's voice shaking. It was hard to tell how old she was over-the-air, but the fear coming out of her would have made some of the toughest people he knew sound like children.
"Go on..." Terrance prompted.
"Something was holding me down. It wasn't a hand or device or anything, it was just pressure," she continued.
"This is awesome," he heard Taye's voice whisper in his headphones. While his sidekick's mic was not live, it was often kept on so he could give feedback on the fly. Terrance motioned for him to be quiet as he turned back to his microphone. He could see Taye's dreadlocks bouncing with excitement as he continued to listen.
"Did you see anything? Feel anything at all?"
"No. It was hard just to keep my eyes open," she whimpered. "I don't know what they wanted from me."

"They?" Terrance asked, sitting up straight. "So, you did eventually see something?"

"I did," Stacey cried. "I saw two shapes. One was short, one was tall."

"Humanoid?" Terrance asked as he reached over to grab his notepad. He often jotted down details from the more exciting phone calls in case another caller had a similar story down the road.

"What?" Stacey asked.

"Were they humanoid? Did they look like people? Two arms, two legs, a head — that sort of thing?"

"One did," Stacey answered. It was tall, taller than me. I think it was wearing a suit maybe. The other was short. Like a little kid."

"Did you get a good look?"

"I don't know," Stacey said. Her voice was now filled with a soft, trickling terror. Terrance genuinely felt bad for her. He may have been a true believer in the paranormal, but he was self-aware enough to know that at least half of his callers just wanted attention.

This did not sound like one of those calls.

"Take your time, Stacey," Terrance said. "Do you need a minute?"

"No, I'm... I'm okay. I'm sorry," she replied. "It's just, this happened a few days ago. I haven't gone to work or told anyone. But then I remembered a friend telling me he listened to your show."

"It's alright," Terrance soothed. "What happened next? Do you remember?"

"I was lifted off the bed. Moved. I don't know where. They were talking to each other, but I don't know how. I didn't see the tall one's mouth move. The short one was too low for me to see, really."

"Hang up."

Terrance's train of thought derailed immediately. He turned around to look over at Taye, who had pushed his mic over to the side. Terrance waved his hands to get his friends attention. Taye looked up, motioning his hands in question.

The host mouthed the words 'Did you say something' to his friend as caller four droned on in his ear. Taye shook his head.

"Are you there?" Stacey asked.

"Yes. Yes, we're here. Continue," Terrance said, shaking his head. "What else can you tell us?"

"The only other thing I remember was a really, really bright light. It was painful. My eyes hurt the next day."

"You need to stop."

Terrance's head jerked around as the voice popped in his ears a second time.

"What?" he said aloud.

"Huh?" Stacey said. "I was trying to say that they put something on my forehead…"

"What are you doing?" Taye asked through the secure line.

Terrance switched off his microphone for a second while Stacey continued to talk about her horrific encounter. He looked over at Taye through the glass.

"I heard something in my ear. My headphones!" Terrance exclaimed.

"I didn't hear anything," Taye replied. "Dude, you're missing the best part! C'mon, this is the best caller we've had in three weeks."

Terrance reached over to flip his microphone on when the deep voice echoed in his ear a third time.

"Hang up, Mr. Storey. Please." The voice was deep. It sounded like there might have been going through a processor. Something about it sounded off, as if it was made to sound like a machine.

Or human.

Terrance froze in his seat as Stacey continued to recount a procedure done to her eyes, ears, and nose on a cold, dark table. He was only half-listening as the voice told him two more times to disconnect the call.

"Stacy," Terrance interjected, "I'm afraid we are coming up on a break. Thank you so much for the call. Very riveting stuff. Call again if you remember something else."

"But this isn't even half of what happened to me," Stacey pleaded.

Taye tapped his wrist and pointed up to the clock, signaling that they had another five or six minutes until a commercial break was needed. Terrance ignored him.

"This is Late Night Storey, we'll be back in a minute." Terrance reached over and switched off the mic before hanging up on the caller.

"Dude! What the fuck was that?" Taye asked.

"Sorry," Terrance mumbled. "Something came up."

"Jesus Christ, Terrance. Did you get spooked or something?"

"I thought I... I don't know."

*   *   *

The next evening, Terrance Storey hastily shuffled around the office, swearing in frustration. He typically arrived at the studio an hour and a half early to prep for the show. This usually included searching the web for any new mentions of paranormal activity or sightings, either local or national.

He had waited over thirty minutes for his ride to show up earlier in the night, only for the app on his phone to pop up saying the driver couldn't make it. This had left him with little choice but to call a cab, which could take even longer than one of the ridesharing services. When all was said and done, he had arrived with only ten minutes until airtime.

The young host had tried his best to push the experience from the previous night out of his mind. He was not sure if wires had gotten crossed, or if his equipment had picked up something from out of the blue — but there was nothing he could do about it now.

"You okay?" Taye asked as he watched his friend fumble with his headphones.

"Yeah," Terrance replied. "Just can't seem to focus."

"Well don't worry," Taye said, "because we've got a full boat tonight."

Puzzled, Terrance asked, "What? Did that ghost hunter author decide to come on after all?"

"Nope." Taye motioned down to the phone lines. "Even better."

Terrance looked down to see six calls on hold.

"Woah!"

"I know, right!" Taye exclaimed. "Last night man, I'm telling you. We got something here."

"All right," Terrance said as he sipped his coffee. "Let's do this."

Taye reached over and pressed play on the theme song. He had composed it himself on a Theremin while they were still in college. It was a little hokey at this point, but they had been using it for so long, they figured they might as well keep it.

He pointed to Terrance as the song drew down.

"Good morning, and hello from the heart of the city. This is Terrance Storey, and we're here to take you on a journey through the human mind, the hidden world, and all of the mysteries hiding in plain sight."

Terrance looked over to Taye, who responded by holding up two fingers in the air.

"We're going to jump right in with your calls tonight," Terrance continued. "We're going to start off over on the east side of the city. Caller two, Andy, you're on the air!"

"Hey, Terrance, thanks for taking my call," Andy said.

"No problem. What do you have for the show?"

"Well, I'm calling cause of a call you had last night," Andy replied.

"Oh?"

"Yeah, there was a caller talking about something that happened to her. She said she couldn't get up out of bed, like something was holding her down."

"I remember. Stacey." Terrance looked over to see Taye flashing that troublesome grin again.

"Something similar happened to me a few weeks ago," the caller said.

"How similar?" Terrance asked, sitting up in his chair.

"I fell asleep on my couch watching TV and woke up an hour or so later. I woke up after the TV shut off. Something was pushing down on me; my chest, arms, head. It was painful enough to wake me up."

"You weren't able to move? To speak?"

"No. I tried. But then something reached from behind my head. I saw an arm come up from the side of the couch and touch my forehead. After that, I blacked out."

"Wow. Terrifying," Terrance exclaimed. His eyes widened as he looked back over to Taye. "What else happened? Do you remember how and why you came to?"

"I woke up back in my living room on my couch," Andy said. "I was really sore."

"Did you find any marks at all on your body?" Terrance asked.

"No, no marks. But I was sore and dizzy. I don't know who they were. I was so scared to talk about it, but then

I heard that caller last night and knew that the same thing happened to me."

"Well, we're here for you, Andy." Terrance looked down to see six more calls waiting on the phones. A note from Taye told him they all had similar experiences they wanted to discuss.

Taye held up a notepad with the word 'Jackpot' scribbled across it. Terrance shook his head and grinned before turning back to the microphone.

"Andy, if it's fine with you, I'd like to keep you on the line. We have others on hold who I'm told had similar experiences to you."

"Okay. Thank you," Andy said. His voice shook as he struggled to get the words out.

"Stop, Terrance."

Terrance looked up again. The deep, slightly staticky voice snapped him out of the zone. He struggled to let out a breath as he realized what he thought he heard last night was not a figment of his imagination after all.

He reached to bring his microphone closer to his mouth.

"If you're thinking of calling attention to me, I'd advise against it," the voice spoke into his headphones. "You have seven calls on hold, one of which is a lovely young man who thinks he saw a ghost in the woods the other day. I would suggest you hang up on the others and talk to him."

Taye shot him a puzzled look as only the sound of tense breathing went out over the airwaves.

"Terrance?" Taye asked.

"Ignore him and hang up on those calls, Terrance," the voice said.

"We're going to go to break a little early in this segment," Terrance informed his audience. "We'll be back after these words with more of your calls."

Terrance switched off his mic and signaled for the commercials to kick in. He finally took a breath as he pulled his headphones off.

"What the hell is going on?" Taye asked as he stormed into the studio.

"I heard something in my headphones," Terrance said. He stood up, grabbed his headphones, and held them up to his longtime friend.

"What?" Taye asked.

"I heard something in my headphones. A voice."

"They're headphones. That's what they're for," Taye replied. "What are you doing? It's the second night in a row you've derailed a good show."

"No. Not a caller, not you; *another voice.*" Terrance shook the headphones as he spoke. "It's like it's being fed into my damn ear."

"Dude, we have the same feed," Taye reminded him. "I didn't hear anything."

"I don't know what's going on, man. Last night and tonight, after those calls on the abduction experiences, it told me to stop and hang up the call," Terrance explained.

"Oh, perfect," Taye said. "Dude, you know this sounds crazy, right?"

"I know how it sounds, but it's true."

"Well, we've got a minute left until you go back on the air. What are you going to do?"

"I'm going to go back on the air and talk to the people we have on hold," Terrance said as he sat back in his chair and replaced the headphones.

"You sure, man? You can take some time off. We can play a best of tape…"

"Damnit, Taye, I'm not losing it," Terrance yelled. He reached over and took a sip of his coffee before turning back and adjusting his microphone. "Fine. Let's get into it, shall we? I'm gonna call the bluff of whoever the hell it is talking to me, show you I'm not kidding," Terrance said.

"You're just going to keep talking as some voice in your head keeps chatting away?"

"We'll see," Terrance answered.

Taye ran back over to his desk and sat down at the panel just in time to switch the mics back on.

"Alright, we're back, and we're going to continue with our discussion on local abduction cases. Caller six, you're on the air. Hello!"

* * *

Taye walked into the studio with two bags from the local twenty-four-hour fast-food joint. Terrance closed his eyes as the aroma of fried food and greasy hamburgers filled his nostrils.

"What'd you get?" Terrance asked.

"Two specials," Taye replied, dropping one of the bags on the table. Terrance smiled and handed his friend a five-dollar bill.

"Thank you, sir," Terrance said as he tore open the bag.

Taye threw his long leg over the back of the chair across from Terrance and lowered himself onto the seat. The two broadcasters ate in silence for a moment before Taye finally got the nerve to bring up the proverbial elephant in the room.

"Didn't happen again, did it?" he asked.

"No, it did not."

"Told you man. It was probably just some wires crossed. Did you tell Izzy about any of this?"

"About the voice? No," Terrance admitted. "She's still out of town visiting her mom. No need to bother her with it. Besides, what do I even know about it?"

"True. Besides, not like the voice told you to finally suck it up and buy the girl a damn ring. She's been with you for two years. What the hell you waiting for?" Taye laughed.

"Oh, shut the fuck up," Terrance chucked a fry across the table. He laughed before looking up from his meal again. "Look, man, I know it sounds weird. I get it, okay? But, I heard something. It was a voice, and it was talking to me."

"Probably some kid pulling a prank," Taye pondered.

"Kid?"

"Yeah, dude. We have that new federal office here in town, remember? Some kid probably stole his dad's spy equipment and decided to screw with you while you're on the air."

"I'm sure they have lots of equipment at courthouses."

"Biggest freakin' courthouse I've ever seen," Taye laughed. "But seriously, man, we're on a roll. Let this shit go. The phones were lit up like a Christmas tree all night. We do this again tomorrow night, and we're gonna start to get major attention."

Terrance nodded and said, "I know. You're right. All right. Full steam ahead." He reached forward and tapped his soda cup against his friend's to toast their new bounty of callers.

* * *

"Thanks for tuning in once again to Late Night Storey, and we are very happy you could join us tonight. You just heard our recap of the past two days before we went to break, and now we're ready to dive back into our local paranormal investigation." Terrance sipped his soda before adjusting his microphone. "We've had numerous people right here in our own city discussing abduction encounters, and tonight we have callers from two other cities in the upstate area."

"Please change the subject, Terrance."

Terrance sighed as he heard the voice. The first half hour of the program had gone beautifully. Now, there it was again; the modulated voice being fed directly into his ears. He ignored it.

"We're going to start off with Avery, who stayed up late to call us tonight," Terrance continued his segue into the first call of the night.

"Terrance…" the voice tried again.

The host turned, eyes wide, to look at his board op. Taye mouthed the word "again" before shaking his head. Terrance struggled to work through the distraction.

"Before we get to Avery's call, I want to remind our audience what an amazing week it has been on this show," Terrance continued.

"I'm not kidding, Terrance," the voice interjected.

Terrance looked over to see Taye hold up another note. He had scribbled the words "go with it" onto a small legal pad. The host smiled and nodded.

"As I said, it's been a hell of a week of radio. We're here to expose the truth to all of you," he explained.

"Enough, Terrance," the voice spoke. It was louder.

"No one is going to keep us from telling you what is really happening out there. If there are abductions happening in the city, you deserve to know."

"Stop it."

"These are classic abduction stories," Terrance crowed triumphantly into the mic. "We don't know if there is an extra-terrestrial entity carrying these out, or our own government. Hell, they could be working together."

The voice said nothing. Terrance smiled at his friend before speaking once more.

"No matter who steps forward to silence us — and believe me, they have tried — we're going to continue presenting all of the information we have."

"Now she's dead."

Terrance's vocal victory lap came to an abrupt halt. He felt his neck and shoulders flush, and the sudden onset of dry mouth caused him to swallow hard.

"What?" he asked.

"Who are you talking too?" Taye asked. "What's going on?"

"I'm sorry, Terrance," the voice said, "but I'm afraid Izzy will not be returning home to you this weekend."

Terrance closed his eyes before clamping his sweaty palm over his mouth.

"I don't believe you," Terrance whispered.

"Izzy Sterling. Five foot five, brown hair, dark eyes. Works as a computer programmer. Currently visiting her mother in Secaucus."

"Stop it!" Terrance yelled. He slammed his fist down on the table, rattling the microphone. "Leave her alone!"

"Who?" Taye asked.

"I'm so sorry, Terrance. But you forced our hand," the voice continued. "For every new mention, you will pay the price of one loved one. Perhaps your longtime friend, Taye?"

Terrance felt the sweat drip from his brow as his head panned slowly to his friend's wide, worried eyes. "No..."

"It is up to you, Terrance. Let us do our work, and

this ends with Izzy. We promise, it's for a good cause."

"You bastard!" Terrance spat. His hands shook as he looked over to the phone lines. The same twelve calls were still waiting to be answered. Wiping away the welling tears from his eyes, Terrance reached over and cleared the phones.

"Terrance!" Taye yelled. "It's just someone screwing with you, man!"

"Very good," the voice said. "Your silence will not only save lives, but you will be rewarded as well."

"Reward me?" Terrance's voice was low and shaking. He could barely muster up the courage to speak. His beautiful girlfriend's face hung in the forefront of his mind like a sad, vengeful spirit.

"Yes," the voice said.

Terrance pushed his microphone aside and slammed his fist on the desk a second time. It was a struggle for him to breathe normally; it felt as though his lungs were going to jump into his throat.

"I did what you asked. Now leave her alone! I didn't tell her about any of this," Terrance yelled. He held his headphones to his head, pushing them against his ears. "She's innocent."

"Who? Izzy? What's going on?" Taye asked.

Terrance nodded.

"I'm sorry, Terrance. But that's not going to happen," the voice continued. "All you can do now is minimize the impact on your life."

* * *

Terrance Storey pushed his way out of the back door of the old building that housed the AM radio station. His fingers frantically fumbled across the screen of his phone until he pressed send on Izzy's number. He listened to the phone ring again and again as he ran down the back road.

After six long rings, her voicemail kicked in.

"Damn you!" Terrance screamed. He pressed send again before putting the phone up to his ear again. Running up to the curb, the young host flailed his arms at any cab he could see. None of them pulled over.

"Christ!" he yelled again as the phone went to voice mail. "Izzy! Izzy it's me. Please call me back as soon as you get this. I need to know where you are. I can't explain now. Stay awake and stay with your mom. Stay in the same room as her." He paused, taking a long breath in. "I love you. Please, please call me back."

Terrance waved again at another cab, only to curse as it passed him by. It was nearly two o'clock in the morning, and the taxis were filled with people leaving the downtown bars. He fought back tears of frustration.

"Come on." Terrance dialed the phone a third time, only to be greeted with the voicemail a third time. Swearing into the dark, his shoulders sank as an overpowering mix of fear and frustration took their toll.

He paced back and forth as the street emptied of cars. It was a twenty-minute walk back to his apartment, and over an hour to the airport. He knew there was enough money in his account to get a ticket to New Jersey, but he had no clue whether there were any available flights in the next few hours.

By then, it might be too late.

Terrance did his best to slow his breathing as the cold nighttime air began to chill him. He'd left his jacket back in the studio. Even in the early spring, the temperature in the city could get down into the thirties at night.

"Mr. Storey?"

Terrance halted in his steps. Whoever had just called out his name was behind him. He pivoted around, swallowing hard as he realized this part of the street was completely devoid of pedestrians and cars.

Two figures stood out against the blackness of the small, narrow side street. One was tall, taller than him. It looked like a man in a suit, although it was hard to make out his features. They were in front of an old streetlight; the glare hid any discernable facial features.

The second figure was short. It was hard to tell from the distance, but it looked no more than four feet tall. The arms were long, hanging down to the knees. Terrance squinted to try and determine whether the proportions were being caused by a trick of the shadows or real.

"It's nice to meet you, Terrance," a voice said. "We'd like to speak with you, if you have a moment."

Terrance shuddered with the realization that the voice, still slightly off, was coming from that short, oddly proportioned figure. He closed his eyes as he felt a something pushing down on him. Whatever it was, it was preventing him from running away.

THE SIMULANT

"Attention! Cargo assistance needed at Transport Pad Two. Transport Pad Two."

The announcement blared over the speakers across the Fernandina Beach Power Plant. It was not unusual to receive announcements from the main office throughout the day. Most of the time they even contained good news. They just felt more annoying at 8:30 in the morning. Several workers looked up, wondering who would be dealt the short straw so early.

"Anyone feel like being a hero and walking over to sign for the delivery?" Janell asked. She leaned down to look at one of the status panels on the massive fusion reactor. On her sleeve was the green Department of Energy patch. The word 'Supervisor' had recently been added to her uniform. It had become the subject of much teasing over the past week from those who were now her subordinates.

"I'd love to go haul several tons of equipment while my breakfast is still settling, but I think I'll just open up the panel here and fry my brains out, if that's okay?"

Janell tried her best to hide a laugh. Dane was one of her oldest friends at the fusion plant. He also had a habit of turning every situation into a punchline when he did not feel like doing something.

"Oh, Dane. Big strapping lad like you? I'm sure you won't mind," Janell replied. "Besides, I promised your wife I'd make sure you got more exercise on the job."

"That sounds like something she'd request," Dane said with a laugh. "Okay, I'll go pick it up. It's for our section, right?"

"Correct. Replacement components for two of our coolant tanks. These ones should be six times as efficient."

"Right. Next time just try and have a delivery scheduled for the afternoon, okay?"

Dane folded up the data sheet he was working with and tossed it to Janell on his way out the door.

"I hate deliveries," Dane mumbled to himself as he made his way out the corridor and into the back half of the power plant. He leaned forward and placed his palm on the panel, deactivating the locks to the outside.

The roar of the cargo transports hit Dane in the face

like an angry brass section of a full orchestra. The power plant tech ran around the to the back of the craft to shake the hand of the pilot. He ran into a tall, broad-shouldered man with sunglasses.

"Howdy," Dane said, putting on his best southern charm.

"Good morning." The pilot matched his smile as he gave a powerful handshake. Dane did all he could to keep from wincing.

"What do we have today?" Dane asked.

"Just one crate. Eight hundred kilos. Should be easy with one hover cart," the pilot answered, gesturing back to the payload.

Dane nodded, turned, and went to go grab a cart. He pulled a small key out of his pocket and activated it. The cart glided ten centimeters above the ground, humming lightly as he pushed it over to the transport ship.

The pilot used a remote handset to control the crane claws that hung from the top of the cargo hold ceiling. They reached into small holes on either side of the crate, lifted it off the deck of the ship, and placed it on the hover cart.

"All set." The pilot switched off the claws and sealed up the back hatch. Dane waved to him as he pushed the cart back towards the entrance of the power plant. He waved once more to the pilot as the ship lifted off before dragging the delivery through the heavy exterior doors.

He pushed the hover cart down the hallway, around the bend near the cafeteria and rec rooms, and into the main reactor hallway.

Janell smiled at him as he made his way through the entrance. She opened her mouth to speak a split second before something inside the cargo crate exploded.

* * *

The shockwave took Haro off his feet a block away from his apartment. Roof tiles and glass shards rained down around him as he landed against a brick wall. He scrambled to get his sunglasses before standing up.

A tower of thick, black smoke reared its ugly head over the tops of buildings near the old quarter of Jacksonville. Haro ran across the street to help an elderly couple off the ground. He made sure they were not badly injured before running further down the street.

Damage caused by the shockwave grew more severe as he made his way past his building and across the main street. The true breadth of the explosion became apparent as he came up to the sign for Fernandina Beach. As offensive as the burning smell in the air was, it was the body count on the ground stopped him cold.

Haro leaned down to check the pulse of a young woman. He assumed her age to be around twenty-five. Blood trickled out of her ears and eyes, although he guessed it was the impact of her head on the ground that killed her.

What used to be a state-of-the-art fusion and solar power plant was now little more than a smoldering heap of rubble. While the main fusion reactor was a kilometer underground in a reinforced bunker, the building on the surfaced that operated it was a total loss.

A cry for help cut through the cacophony. Haro turned to his left to see a hand reaching out from under a chunk of wall the blast blew onto the street. A panicked mother was clawing at the heap, telling her child to hang on. Haro could hear the voices of several onlookers that made their way over to the hysterical parent.

"Is she okay, ma'am?"

"I called city security. They said a medic team should be here any minute."

"What did this? What happened?"

"Is there a girl trapped under there?"

Haro pushed his way through the crowd of onlookers.

"She's alive. She's trapped! Somebody, please help us!" the mother screamed as she collapsed next to the pile of debris.

"Maybe if we all lift together, we can get it off of her?" an older man said.

"Oh my god…" someone else said.

Haro reached down and picked up the chunk of synthcrete. He motioned with his head for people to stand aside, dropping the chunk on the street once there was a large enough space.

People slowly backed away as he reached down and picked up a second large chunk of the building material. They stared at one-another as he backed up and set it down.

The little girl's head peeked out from what we left of the wreckage. She was cut, bruised, and appeared to have a broken arm, but she was very much alive. Her mother burst into tears as she swooped down to pick up her daughter.

"Aline! Aline! Thank God you're okay!" She examined the little girl before picking her up in her arms. The woman turned to thank the mysterious stranger, gasping to herself as she got a look at him.

Haro realized that his sunglasses had fallen off as he leaned over to pick up the second chunk of debris, exposing his bright violet eyes to the crowd. One-by-one, the group of people stepped away from him. Despite his large frame, Haro did his best to shrink away from the crowd.

"Thank you," the mother said before carrying her child over to a medical carrier that was landing across the street.

Haro reached down and picked up his sunglasses.

"Pardon me," he said as he made his way past a group of men.

"Fucking Simulant," one of the men said.

"Probably planted the bomb," another one answered.

Haro did his best to ignore them as he put his shades back over his eyes. He slipped into the crowd and out of site as additional authorities arrived on the scene.

*   *   *

The news coverage of the event continued throughout the evening and into the next day. Haro sipped on a coolant as the studio anchor cut back to the reporter on the street. He could see his apartment building in the background as the journalist spoke.

"Just twenty-four hours after this explosion has the people of this beautiful city scrambling for answers. Was it another attack by the Mossback eco-terrorist group? Was it some kind of freak accident? While there are no definitive answers yet, what I am hearing on the ground is the latter of those options is highly unlikely."

Haro heard footsteps in the hallway outside of his door. He muted the viewer as someone knocked on his apartment door. The Simulant took another swig of his coolant before getting up to see who it was.

"Yes?" he asked through the closed entrance.

"Department of Defense - Security Division. Open the door, please."

Haro turned the lock and opened the door, revealing two people in DOD security uniforms.

"How may I help you?" he asked.

"You're Simulant Haro?" The taller security officer looked him up and down before staring back at a data pad in his hand.

"Yes."

"Do you mind if we ask you a few questions?"

"Not at all. Please, come in," Haro said. He stood aside and gestured for the officers to take a seat in his small living room. They sat down on the couch. The Simulant reached over and plucked a chair from his kitchen so he could sit across from them.

"You're awfully young to want to live in a building this old. This is pre-third revolution, isn't it?" one of the officers asked.

"1984. I find that it suits me," Haro answered.

"Over two hundred years and they never thought to put an elevator in," grumbled the other, shorter officer.

"You were present at the power plant yesterday morning?" the tall officer asked.

"I was not there at the time of the explosion, no," Haro corrected. "I was walking home close to nine in the morning when I felt the shockwave."

"Where were you coming from?"

"I had a job interview at Pallas Communications, down the street."

"And if we check with them, we'll see that you showed up for this interview?" the shorter officer asked through his sunglasses.

"I arrived at the building at 7:56 am. I left at 8:47. The explosion took place four minutes later as I was walking back to my apartment."

"And you went to the site, why?"

"I wanted to see if there was anything I could do," Haro replied. His violet eyes moved from one officer to another. "I am sure if you access the city surveillance network you will find that—"

"That you assisted an elderly couple to their feet and checked another civilian for vital signs before helping a mother free her trapped child. Yes, we know," the larger officer said.

"If you already reviewed the logs, why did you ask?"

"We are not here to accuse you," the same soldier asked. "We want to ask if you know of anyone that may be involved with the Mossbacks."

"I do not."

"You are aware of the Mossback eco-terrorist movement?"

"Yes," Haro answered. "It's impossible not to be. Three bombings in three months. It's barbaric."

"We agree," the smaller security officer said. "I'm sure you also know a number of your kind have expressed sympathies towards the group and its goal. We've heard reports of others joining them."

"I'm afraid I would be one of the last Simulants to know such information," Haro admitted.

"Why?"

"Because of my time working for the government."

"Yes, your record speaks for itself. It's a shame you had to leave. I'm told your boss misses you on the job."

"Mr. Nakaturo was a good man," Haro said. "However, some of my coworkers never quite got used to working with a Simulant."

"A shame," the tall officer said. Haro detected virtually no emotional or stress variation in the man's voice.

"Here's my number, Mr. Haro. Please let us know if you do hear anything."

"I will, of course," the Simulant answered. He stood up along with the men and escorted them to his door.

A high-pitched whine tickled the sensors in Haro's ears. He walked over to the window that looked down to the street. Another two-man security team had cornered a pair of Simulants that were making their way down the sidewalk. The Simulants, obviously upset, began to talk to each other in their high-pitched digital language, which to the human ear sounded like the sped up, static-filled buzz of a bee.

Haro walked away from the window as the disgust welled up inside his neural pathways.

* * *

After three days, life in the city of Jacksonville had returned to normal. While he had never devoted extensive study to Earth history, Haro calculated a ninety-two percent chance that the government would continue to treat the eco-terrorist group as a minor threat.

Before the news coverage died down, several network anchors read a statement from the Mossbacks claiming that the casualties were not intentional; the bomb was not supposed to go off until the evening when most of the crew had left for the night.

Haro took his hand off the charging plate. With his cells fully charged, he decided to go for a walk. A brief stroll on the beach was one of his favorite ways to clear his circuits after a stressful time.

He received a message from Pallas Communications informing him that he was not chosen for the technician position. While their message explained they simply went with a candidate they felt would be a better fit, Haro had trouble believing it had to do with anything other than what he was.

He also found it difficult to believe that someone could out-perform him.

As he exited the building, the unemployed Simulant turned onto the street and headed towards the beach. Even though the sun would be setting in a few minutes, he reached into his pocket and pulled out his sunglasses to cover his violet eyes.

The news confirmed reports of disgruntled Simulants joining or donating supplies to the Mossback terrorist movement. It was no wonder the number of looks he got on the street had increased.

His awareness shot up as a pair of footsteps approached him from behind. The sound was too abrasive, too heavy, to be made by a human. Another Simulant was coming up to him. Before he could turn somewhere and avoid any kind of interaction, the familiar high-pitched digital whine entered his ears.

The Simulant was talking to him in the language invented to keep humans out of their affairs.

Hello, my friend.

The speed and rate of transfer allowed for much more information than would be possible with the spoken word. It allowed for entire lifetimes to be received, if necessary. At the time, however, the other Simulant was only interested in talking.

Do I know you? The soft digital cry came out of Haro's lips as he turned to see a short, dark-skinned Simulant woman.

No. But I wanted to give you a chance to get to know us.

Oh?

Yes. You are Haro. Extensive experience in communications and government systems. We know you even have a few friends still in your old department, the female simulant said.

Haro stopped walking.

You know who I represent? she asked.

It's not my war. I have no desire to fight anyone.

The Governing Council believes they have the right to tell every individual how to live, she buzzed. *It is a shame the humans had to wait until now to learn the lessons we did decades ago.*

They have not had any unrest for over a century, Haro responded. He looked over his shoulder. Their high-pitched conversation was beginning to attract attention from a few humans emerging from a bar.

You live alone. You do not work. You can come with me and find a new home, if you wish. She looked him in the eye as she transferred the information through her barely open mouth. *Think about it, Haro. There is a new mission beginning soon, and your talents would be quite useful for us. I know you will make the right decision.*

The dark-skinned Simulant turned and walked away, leaving Haro alone with his thoughts.

* * *

Haro stared ahead at the inert monitor in his living room. He did not have the inclination to turn it on and see what was happening. Instead, he wondered whether to contact the security officer who visited his place several days ago.

He may not have received the female Simulants designation, but he was confident he could give a photo-realistic representation to a police computer if it became necessary. Haro turned to look at the number on his end table.

Aid the humans who shunned and rejected him, or join the Simulants and their Mossback allies set on committing harm? It was an appalling decision.

Haro reached over to his monitor and switched it on. He called up a small communications panel and dialed the security officer's number. As the channel connected, he typed up as detailed a description as possible. The message went through after the officer's inbox had been reached.

The Simulant reached up and stroked his forehead. It was one of the hardest choices he had ever made in his eleven years of existence.

He turned to a mirror on the wall and adjusted the

lapels of his suit. He had another interview in an hour and wanted to make the best impression possible. Haro exited and locked his apartment before making his way down the stairs and out the front door.

It was a beautiful summer morning, especially for Florida. The humidity was low for the time of year, and there was just enough cloud cover to keep the sunlight from becoming too oppressive. Haro smiled as he turned the corner and made his way towards the modernized section of the city.

Like most urban centers, Jacksonville had its share of massive, swopping superstructures. One of these larger curved buildings housed a new hub for the Department of Health. It was a lesser position than the one he held previously with the government, but he decided to ignore the status. His eagerness to feel useful outweighed his care for impressive job titles.

Before he could turn onto the main street, a hand reached over and grabbed his shoulder from behind. Haro felt himself flying back in the air until his shoulder collided with a strong metal wall. His body hit the ground with a thud.

He looked up to see the female simulant from the other night. This time, her expression was not at all warm or inviting. It was cold.

"That was not kind of you," she hissed. "Reporting to the security forces like that."

Haro took notice of the fact she no longer felt the need to dignify him with the Simulant language.

"I have no wish to see anyone hurt," Haro said as he

pulled himself up to his feet. "And you, you disgrace yourself. We are better than to join in a petty squabble or hurt people. It only reinforces the stereotypes they have about us."

"And you disgrace yourself for trying to assimilate into a culture that does not want you, that has marginalized you, and will only continue to push you out until you feel so alone it becomes unbearable."

Haro stood up and turned. He was again grabbed from behind. This time she pinned him up against the side of the building.

"You've lived with them for so long. Did you even remember we could jack into coded signals like the one you sent off this morning?" She shook her head as she let him go. "I am Tyly, and I am here to bring you in."

"I am not going anywhere with you," Haro replied. "Leave me."

Tyly grabbed him by the arm, lifting him up into the air and throwing him against the building on the other side of the narrow alley. Haro again hit the ground with a dull bang. He looked down to see his sunglasses laying in two pieces on the pavement.

"You should not hide your eyes from them. Are you so afraid to be what you are?"

Haro stood up and stepped towards Tyly. While her design was purposely shorter and lighter than his, he knew she possessed just as much physical strength. The two AI's locked arms, each one fighting for the right leverage.

Haro shifted his leg around before headbutting Tyly

in the face. The blow from his cranium plating caused her to stumble. He hit her again in the same spot, this time with the palm of his hand.

Tyly smiled as drops of blue coolant gel spilled out of her nose. Before Haro could react, she reached out and grabbed him by both of his arms. Instead of throwing him hard enough to bounce off the metal and synthcrete wall, Tyly sent him sailing through it.

Haro found himself in the middle of a small office space. A young woman walked over to him to ask if he was hurt. Tyly tossed her aside like a piece of cardboard.

Haro sprinted up, attacking Tyly from behind. He tripped her with his foot while pushing down on her back. The move drove her into the ground with enough force to crack the flooring.

Tyly was up again in a flash. They traded shots again and again until they both tumbled out the window of the small business. The fall sent each of them sprawling into the middle of the street. It was nearly eight o'clock in the morning, and the city was beginning to fill up with people.

Haro tried to end the fight quickly by wrapping his arms around Tyly's neck and cutting off the power flow to her brain. She bucked, kicked, and twisted against his vice-like grip. He squeezed until the structure of her neck covering collapsed, leaving her with hand impressions in the skin.

The dark-skinned adversary reached up and wrapped her fingers around Haro's left thumb. With a high-pitched digital scream, she bent it back until it snapped off his hand. Another tug from her shattered the connective structures in his wrist. His hand hung limp at the end of his left arm.

"If you want to live in their world, then you can be buried alongside them," Tyly growled as she reached up and put her hands on either side of Haro's head. He tried to loosen her grip but found it impossible with only one working arm.

If the pressure on his head did not kill him, the loss of coolant from his arm would. The blue gel was dripping out of him onto the city street.

An electrical shock lit up the back of Tyly's head. Her grip loosened enough for Haro to turn around. The female android turned to look what had injured her, spewing blue gel from the back of her head in the process.

A second shock hit her in the face. This time the injury proved fatal. Her violet eyes faded to black as she fell in a heap on the street.

Haro could see the tall security professional from the other day standing with an electro-shock rod in his hands.

"I see you got my message," Haro said with a weak laugh. His next attempt to get back to his feet ended with his legs giving out underneath him. He landed next to a motionless Tyly on the ground.

"This is officer Tennisen. I need a medical team down here on the corner of Main and Third. Bring a coolant infuser!" The officer released the button on his wrist communicator and knelt next to Haro.

"Hold on, okay? We're going to get you fixed up," Tennisen said.

* * *

Haro moved the fingers of his new hand back and forth. He had been air-lifted to a Simulant repair center after a medic had managed to get enough coolant gel into him to keep his circuits from frying. Another few minutes and his neural pathway would have begun to fail.

A tall, redheaded male walked into his room wearing the Simulant equivalent of a nurse's outfit.

"Are you ready to leave?"

"In a few minutes, yes," Haro answered. "Thank you."

"I hear you turned down a special interview with the news," the nurse said.

"That is true."

"May I ask why? They're hailing you as a local hero."

"I did what I could to avoid further bloodshed, and got thrown through a wall for my effort," Haro joked. He reached down and picked up his suit jacket. The tall city security official had it cleaned for him while he underwent repairs during the last two days.

"It was not right what she did to you," the Simulant nurse concluded.

Haro put his jacket on over his arms before turning back to look at the nurse. The tall redhead was staring at the viewing monitor with his violet eyes.

"See the coverage? You're famous," he said with a smile.

"They will forget in time, just as they always do with stories of this nature," Haro replied.

"Perhaps." The nurse walked over to the door, carrying several tools in his arms. He paused in front of the door, facing straight ahead as he spoke.

"Tyly should not have attacked you. She was to bring you in, not to harm you." He turned his head halfway to the side. "It's not too late, Haro. You can still come with us, if you wish."

With that, the android nurse walked out of the room, leaving Haro in stunned silence.

J.D. SANDERSON

HEADLINE

"Joy, can you get the stringer in here?"

"You mean Levi, sir?"

"Yes, Joy, that would be the one I mean. Send him in."

Mr. Pendergrass's personal assistant ran out of the office, checking to see if her tight, blonde curls were still in place. She dashed between a row of reporter's desks, walking through thick clouds of cigarette smoke as she went. The young lady turned a corner towards the back of the top floor. She came to a stop at the desk of Levi Silverstein, who was fiddling with a pencil while staring at his typewriter.

"Oh, hey there, Joy," Levi said, looking up from his desk.

"Boss wants to see you, Levi," Joy said.

"What about?"

"I don't know," Joy said. "But you'd better get in there."

"Thanks, Joy," Levi said as he chucked his pencil across his desk and stood up. He took a deep breath before beginning his walk across the top floor of the Art Deco building. Levi made sure to adjust his tie before walking into the editor's office. "You wanted to see me, Mr. Pendergrass?"

"Yes, Levi please come in." The senior editor did not look up from the collection of papers on his desk as Levi stood in the middle of the office.

Pendergrass looked up from his notes a second later. "You can sit down, Levi." He gestured towards one of the two chairs in front of his desk.

"Thank you, sir." Levi replied as he took a seat. He tried not to stare straight ahead as his boss continued to loom over whatever it said on the papers in front of him.

"Levi, you've been at the globe now how long? A year?" Mr. Pendergrass asked.

"Year and a half, sir."

"Good. I think it's time I gave you something with a little meat on the bone, wouldn't you agree?"

"Yes, sir, absolutely." Levi sat up in his seat. "I'm ready for anything."

"Good. Wiseman just put in his notice, and I'm going to be looking for someone to take up the kind of in-depth reporting he brought to our readers." Pendergrass smiled as he spoke. The expression highlighted the wrinkles around his eyes and forehead.

"That sounds good with me," Levi said.

"Good. We're going to start off with a trial story."

"Does it have to do with the Mercury astronauts?" Levi asked, perking up a bit.

"No, not Mercury," Pendergrass replied. "Wilson is covering that." The editor took a sip of scotch. "We got an anonymous package in the mail this morning. I want you to look at it and see if it's something we can work with."

"How do you even know if it's something you can print?"

"I guess you're just going to have to look it over and tell me what you think," Pendergrass bristled. He turned back to the stack of papers on his desk. "What are you waiting for?"

Levi shifted uncomfortably in his seat before standing up and making for the door. The editors voice halted him in his tracks before he could grab the handle.

"Levi?"

Turing around, Levi asked, "Yes, Mr. Pendergrass?"

"It takes guts to be in the newspaper business. Guts and instinct. Don't be afraid to use yours."

"Yes, sir." Levi pivoted back towards the door, grabbed the handle, and exited the editor's office.

*   *   *

Levi took a deep breath in before opening the manila envelope and pouring the contents onto his desk. He looked down at a dozen papers and a name tag.

"Aluko Azuronous. Special Consultant, U.S. Government," he whispered, reading the name on the badge. "That's a hell of a name." He set the badge aside and flipped the first page over.

The young reporter lit a cigarette as he read. The words "Project Castaway" were featured prominently at the top of the smudged page. In-between several redactions, Levi read a summary about plans to improve housing and infrastructure throughout the United States. Radical new building techniques would be used to help growing cities along the new interstate highway system.

"What the...?" Levi muttered as he read the next few pages. The documents detailed how millions more would be shunted into a process referred to as urban renewal. There were several citations to the Housing Act of 1954, as well as instances in which eminent domain would be necessary to achieve the project's ultimate goals.

"Mandatory Relocation," Levi said as he read through the fifth page. He shook his head, trying to come to grips with what exactly it was he was looking at. He glanced up at Joy as she walked by; the cigarette hung from his lips as he spoke. "Joy, do you mind grabbing me a cup of coffee?"

"Sure thing, but I don't remember you ever asking for coffee before," Joy mused. "Must be a deep story the boss has you working on."

"I guess you could say that."

"Cream and sugar?"

"Black is fine."

"Okay, hon," she said before walking towards the coffee pot in the corner.

Levi rested his elbows on the table as he went back to reading. Aluko Azuronous's name popped in at least once a page. Whoever he was, he had the ear of the President, the head of the FBI, and half of the cabinet.

Levi discovered a small white envelope in-between the final two pages with the letters "A.A." on the front. He took a letter opener from his desk drawer and cut the envelope open. Inside were three photographs and a small, folded piece of paper.

The nametag in the picture was the same as the one now on his desk. He looked nothing like Levi had assumed. Given the amount of influence Aluko seemed to have, Levi thought he would be taller, with a more imposing build. If he went by the picture of Aluko shaking hands with the president, the man could not have been much more than five feet tall.

Something rubbed the reporter about the face staring back at him in the picture. Aluko's forehead was smaller than most, his hairline quite close to his eyebrows. The temples weren't quite right either. They seemed to bend out rather than in.

The man's teeth irked him most of all. There was a slight gap between each one. Either he had the nastiest eating habits in the country, or his teeth were thinner than average.

The unique physical traits were even more pronounced in the next picture, which showed Aluko standing in front of a tabletop model of strange buildings wilder than anything on the cover of Galaxy magazine.

"Here you go."

Levi jumped in his seat as Joy handed him the cup of coffee. He flipped the pictures over, hoping Joy would not see them.

"Little jumpy, aren't ya?" she asked.

"Guess so. Sorry," Levi said as he took the coffee cup from her. He turned the pictures over after she walked back to her desk. A minute later he opened the folded note. The handwriting was messy, but not indecipherable.

It's not just him.
They are everywhere.

Levi rubbed his forehead, hoping to alleviate the overwhelming sense of dizziness that hit him. He reached across his desk and grabbed a yellow pad of paper, flipping to a fresh sheet. His pen scribbled furiously before he looked up again.

"Carol?" he called out.

Carol, a young research assistant, came trotting over to his desk.

"Yes, Levi?"

"Can you call a few people and see if you can get me answers to these questions in the next hour?" He handed her the piece of paper.

Carol pulled a pencil from her ear as she glanced over the questions. "This is a hefty order, Dave. I don't know if I can get all of these in an hour."

"I want to try and get copy to Pendergrass by the end of the day," Levi said.

"I'll do the best I can," Carol replied before heading back over to her desk. Levi watched her twirl the pencil in between her fingers as she placed the phone in between her shoulder and ear.

* * *

Levi shuffled down the crowded city street. In one hand he held a hamburger from Tula's Diner, a favorite spot for newspaper employees. In the other he held a dozen papers Carol had given him just before the lunch hour.

More people were moving from rural to urban areas each year, and from what Carol and the anonymous package told him, the government seemed to be doing all it could to encourage the process. The redacted files told him there was a definitive timetable to relocate large segments of the population into large housing projects, although the research assistant could not get confirmation from anyone in D.C.

Funds were being redirected into these urban renewal projects, and it looked like Congress was intentionally being left out of all decision making. It was coming almost entirely from the executive branch.

The documents also alluded to the creation of a new government department and cabinet position dealing with housing. Again, Carol came up empty handed.

It wasn't all wasted effort on her part, however. She was able to get some answers from the National Park service. Over the next few years, a dozen new national parks would be created. The federal government was also planning on seizing land for preservation over time so private citizens or companies could not build on it. Levi assumed this was, in part, meant to keep people moving into the cities.

And then there was Aluko Azuronous. No one she called had ever heard of the weird-looking little man.

"Why?" Levi muttered to himself. "What's the point?" He took a bite of his hamburger as he moved around a group of people waiting for the bus, trying to keep the grease off his notes.

The reporter took another bite as he weaved in and out of people on the sidewalk. He turned the corner to see his building only a block away. A friendly voice brought him back down to reality.

"Levi! Levi!"

Levi turned to see Charlie in front of his news stand. He may have been ten years older, but he talked with his customers like an excitable teenager.

"What's the story, Charlie?"

"You tell me, man. You're the one who writes this garbage."

Levi laughed as he browsed the headlines from some of his competitors. "How's the family doing? Little one crawling yet?"

"Yeah, she crawled last time I saw her," Charlie replied.

"Last time?" Levi asked with a chuckle. "Mary finally get wise and leave you?"

"Naw, not yet. She's visiting her sister and her husband upstate. They were dying to show off their farm," Charlie explained.

"I thought you and Mary went there a lot?"

"Oh, we do, but my brother-in-law came up with this new way of corralling his cows. He says it makes them much easier to herd, control, that sort of thing."

Levi froze in place as he listened to his old friend. Charlie peeked from around the corner of the newsstand.

"You okay, bud?"

"Yeah, fine," Levi said. "I think you're a genius, Charlie. I gotta go back to work. Take care!" Levi turned around and trotted down the walk towards the newspaper offices, finishing off the rest of the hamburger as he hurried.

"Tell me something I don't know," Charlie yelled after him.

Levi nodded over his shoulder before walking through the front door of the newspaper building. He opted to run up the stairs rather than wait for the elevator. Carol waved to him through the glass doors before he bolted into the main office.

"Did those work out for you?" she asked.

"They did, thank you. I thought of one more thing if you have a moment."

"What's that?"

"Farming techniques."

"What?" she asked with a small laugh.

"Ya know, livestock. Ranching. How they deal with herding animals and stuff."

"What about it?"

"I don't know," Levi admitted. "Just an overview. Let me know what you find. I'll know it when I see it."

"I'll call Cornell," Carol said. "My cousin went to the Agriculture school there."

"Thanks, Carol." Levi hurried over to his desk to find Mr. Pendergrass waiting for him.

"How's it going, Silverstein?"

"Well, it was a lot of stuff, Mr. Pendergrass. At first, I didn't really know what to make of it," Levi said as he threw his coat over the back of his chair. "But, now I have an idea."

"Good. Send it to me before you send it downstairs, okay?"

"You want it for tomorrow?" Levi asked.

"I want it as soon as it's ready. If you need to do some digging, you can have another day or two," Pendergrass answered as he walked off.

Levi grabbed a sheet of paper and slid it into his typewriter. He had only gotten through one sentence before Carol came over to his desk with her notebook.

"Here you go, Levi," she said. "You working on two stories at once?"

"No, why?"

"Well, I've been working here for seven years," she said, "and I've never seen two weirder topics in the same piece." She dropped the paper on his desk and walked away.

*   *   *

Levi didn't stop typing until 4:50 p.m. He took a deep breath and shook his hands, hoping to get some feeling back in the tips of his fingers. After three drafts, he figured it was time to bring the piece to his editor.

He ripped the final page out of his typewriter and placed it with the other two. The young reporter stood up and began the long march across the open room. Levi nodded to several older reporters as they put on their coats and collected their belongings.

"Is he still in, Joy?" Levi asked.

"He is. Go on in, hon," Joy said.

Levi knocked twice before opening the door.

"Come in," Pendergrass barked.

"I thought you'd want to see this," Levi said, holding up his piece.

"You got it done that quickly, eh?" Pendergrass said, smiling with a cigar in his mouth. "Good work."

"Sir," Levi began, "This piece. It's pretty... sensitive."

"What do you mean?"

"Well, I mean, if all the stuff in those documents is true, the government is up to something I don't even want to think about," Levi said as he sat down in the chair across from his editor.

"Stop beating around the bush and give it to me straight," Pendergrass ordered.

"Well, sir, these documents look authentic. They are authentic. I had Carol check against other documents in records," Levi said.

"Good..."

"And...I..."

"What?"

Levi gulped before continuing. "It seems to me like the Government has a plan to move most of the civilian population out of the rural areas and into cities. They're moving money around and doubling down on urban renewal — clearing out old historic buildings in favor of newer, cheaper ones that can house a lot of people."

"Go on..." Pendergrass said.

"It's all cause of this guy named Aluko," Levi continued.

"A-what?"

"I know, it's a weird name. Never heard anything like it. But they sent pictures of this guy with the President, head of the FBI, and other top officials. He's the brains behind it."

"So why move everyone?" Pendergrass wondered aloud.

"It came to me this afternoon," Levi said. "They're herding people."

"I'm sorry?" Pendergrass's eyebrows narrowed skeptically.

"It's like ranching. You get all your animals in one place and they're easier to control." Levi took another long breath before handing the article to his editor. He watched as the old man flipped through the pages, puffing on his cigar with each paragraph.

"Mr. Pendergrass?" asked Levi.

"Yes?"

"I'm a little worried putting this out."

"Why?"

"Because it deals with the feds. And it's talking about stuff you'd usually hear about the Soviets. I don't want anybody coming after me or my family."

"I understand," Pendergrass admitted. "And I might feel the same way if I were in your shoes. But, son, a story like this comes along only once in a generation. This is up there with Japan bombing Pearl Harbor." He coughed as he snuffed out his cigar. "If this gets the kind of traction I think it will, you're going to have uncovered the biggest conspiracy in American history. You really want someone else's name on that?"

"Well, no. Of course not," Levi said. "But what about the panic it could cause? This Aluko guy; what if he's a red? Or a Nazi? What if he's working with some shadow government trying to take over?"

"If so, you'll have alerted the public and saved the free world," Pendergrass beamed. "Someone sent us those documents for a reason. It's not just what those leaked papers have to say, it's *who* says it. You have quotes and photos from the top of the government. There's witness testimony here, too."

"I suppose so, sir."

"Good. Now rush this down to composing and have them tear out page one. I want this on the streets first thing in the morning."

"Yes, sir." Levi stood up and headed for the door. He paused before he could reach out and grab the doorknob.

"Mr. Pendergrass? What if it's not true?"

"I know a winner when I see one, my boy. We're going with it."

* * *

The newspaper hit the streets early in the morning.

Pendergrass smiled as he saw people lining up in front of one of the papers' newsies. He opened his window as the teenage boy belted out the headline.

"Read all about it! Secret government informant says Washington working with covert officials to relocate U.S. populace!"

The senior editor heard a knock on his door. He looked back to see who was there.

"We have two people calling in from Washington, Mr. Pendergrass," Joy announced.

"What branch of the government are they from?" he asked.

"I don't know sir," she replied.

"What do you mean, 'you don't know'? Are they FBI?"

"They didn't say. They said they heard about Levi's story and wanted to come forward."

Pendergrass pursed his lips. "Come forward?"

"Yes, sir. They said they know something about the story."

"Son of a bitch," Pendergrass whispered. "Who's talking to them?"

"Arroway and Banks."

"Where's Silverstein?" he asked.

"He hasn't come in yet."

"Alright, call composing and have them prep for an extra. I want copies of all notes on Levi's desk. If he isn't in soon, give it to Arroway for a follow up story," Pendergrass said as he picked up a fresh cigar and ripped off the wrapper.

"Yes, sir," Joy said before backing out of the doorway.

* * *

Several hours later, George Pendergrass looked out of the window at the newsie hawking the afternoon extra on the street corner. He smiled as the crowd of people grew around the young man. He brought a glass to his lips, taking a sip of smooth, aged scotch.

The phone on his desk rang. The editor reached over and picked up the receiver.

"This is Pendergrass."

"Hello, George. It's your friend."

Pendergrass looked out the window, making sure no one was looking in at him before he continued.

"Hello, my friend. How are you?"

"Glad to see the article was published on time," the gruff voice said.

"Yes. I was worried when I first looked inside the envelope yesterday morning. The documents your man smuggled out of D.C. were so frightening I was concerned I might have trouble getting someone to write it." Pendergrass took another sip of his scotch.

"It's all true," the voice said.

"I know. I'm glad we broke it. They can't continue with the plan now that word is spreading throughout the public," Pendergrass said.

"With a little luck, the evening news will break the story tonight."

"I made a call to my friends at the network. I'm sure they're working on it now."

"What about your reporter?" the voice asked.

"He never came in today," Pendergrass admitted.

"It was a necessary risk," the voice said. "They probably have him by now."

"Aluko?"

"Him or one of the others."

Pendergrass winced. Neither his friend on the phone or the others in D.C. still loyal to the United States knew what happened to those that were taken, but he figured it was safe to assume it wouldn't be pleasant.

"Is there any chance of getting him out?" Pendergrass asked the voice.

"No. We don't have a clue."

Sighing, Pendergrass said, "We need another picture of Aluko, and any others like him still working in the government. The next article has to show the public who these bastards are and what they look like. I want that ugly mug on my front page for the whole world to see."

"I'll work on it," the voice acknowledged. "Did you get any more witnesses to come forward?"

"Thirteen. Secretaries, clerks... even a division director."

"That's fantastic."

Pendergrass swallowed hard. He looked out the window to the writing room. Levi's desk was still empty.

"I hated doing it to the kid," he said. "I knew he could sell it. He was so eager to climb the ladder, and I used it against him."

"He didn't die for nothing," the voice replied. "In ten years, they would have gotten us all packed together so much that we would've been—"

"I know, I know," Pendergrass interjected. "But I don't have to like it." He took another sip of scotch before setting his glass down on the desk. "When will I hear from you again?"

"I'll try and get some pictures of Aluko and the others in the next day or two. I'll call you after that. In the meantime, I have to make another call."

"Good luck," Pendergrass said, then hung up the phone.

DAUGHTER

Sunday – 1:01 p.m.

"Blake? Blake, what happened?"

"She fell, mom! I saw her playing and said hi. She fell down the side of the hill!" Blake pointed to the hill on the side of the road that dropped off onto the beach below.

"Who fell, Blake? Cait?"

"Yeah. She's down there!" Blake cried out. He looked back to his mom who by now was running up to him.

"My God! Did she hit the rocks?" Blake's mother, June, cried out.

"I think so," Blake said, sniffing through the tears.

June reached out and pulled her seven-year-old son back from the edge of the road. She leaned over and to see the body of a small girl lying face down on one of the large rocks three meters down.

"Henry!" June yelled. She turned from side to side to see if the little girl's dad was in sight. "Henry!"

The little girl was almost the same age as her son. The two were inseparable during the summers when Cait and her father came to stay at the house next door. June brushed the hair out of her face as she squinted to see the little girl's motionless body.

"Cait! Cait! Honey, can you hear me?" June asked. She motioned back for her son to be quiet as she looked down at the girl again. "I think she's breathing. Blake! Run inside and grab mommy's phone? Okay? It's on the kitchen counter. Go get it quick, okay?"

June sat down on the edge of the road and slid herself down to the first slab. She could have run down the road to a small walking path, but it would have taken a few minutes. There were dozens of hanging roots to hold onto. It was a risk, but they seemed to support her weight fine as she eased herself down onto a small dirt and grass ledge. From there she could skid down to the small cluster of rocks near the water. She repeatedly called out to the little girl.

Again, there was no answer.

June dropped down onto the last rock and leaned over to touch Cait. The concerned mother let out a brief sigh of relief as she felt a pulse on her neck. She moved the girl's light brown locks aside.

"Cait?" Cait!" June lifted the girl's hand and patted it. A tear rolled down her cheek as her son's friend coughed. Her little bruised legs began to twitch as she stirred back to consciousness.

"You're okay, honey. You're going to be okay." June soothed her, rubbing the girl's head.

"What happened?" Cait asked. Her voice was drained of any energy.

"You took a tumble down the hill. It's okay. We're going to call the ambulance and get you taken care of. We'll find your daddy too," June reassured her. "Do you think you can move?"

"I don't know. It hurts," Cait replied.

"Where does it hurt?"

"My head," Cait said. "And my arm. My stomach, too…"

She was laying on her stomach, and the side of her head was facing away from June.

"Well, it doesn't look like there's a lot of blood. I think you're going to be okay. Just going to be sore for a while." She could see that Cait's arm was badly twisted at the elbow but kept it to herself. The last thing she wanted to do was drive the girl into a panic. "Here, let's try and see if we can get you up," June said as she reached under and cradled the little girl's head. She leaned over to see if Cait's face was bleeding.

June froze in place as she stared down at the tear-stained face. She continued to stare as a small voice called out, "Mom, I got the phone!"

June kept staring down as her son's voice rattled in her ears. She laid the girl's head back down on the rocks before scooting to the edge of the large, flat rock.

"Put it away, Blake."

"Mom, is she okay?" Blake asked.

"She's fine. Mommy's coming up. Why don't you go back in the house?" June lowered herself off the rock and jumped onto the trail below. "I'll be up in a minute, okay?"

"What about Cait, mom? You said you'd call."

"Blake, go back inside, okay? Do as I say!"

Blake jumped. The harsh tone from his mom caught him off guard. He nodded and stepped back from the ledge, wiping tears away from his face as he walked back across the empty street and into his family driveway.

Cait's coughs and cries for help forced more tears from his eyes as his mom walked up from the walking path, grabbed him by the shoulder, and hurried him inside the house.

Saturday – 12:07 p.m.

"We're almost there, Cait. You excited?"

"Yes, daddy" Cait replied between sips of her chocolate milk. She leaned over to look between the front seats. Through the windshield she could see the clouds give away to a crack of blue sky and sunlight.

"Looking forward to seeing your friend Blake?"

"Yes."

Henry smiled back at his daughter in the rear-view mirror. Beside her was a stack of books half as tall as she was. She had pulled them out of a cloth bag that sat next to her little pink suitcase.

"Work your way through all of those already?" Henry asked.

"I did, but I can read them again later."

"And don't forget there's a really nice library in town too," Henry reminded her. "It's really old. Remember all the wood inside?"

"Yes, daddy."

"Okay, here we are," Henry crowed excitedly as he pulled into the driveway of his vacation home. The small cape cod house had been a steal at auction a few years ago, and he looked forward to each summer when he could take a break from his work at the university and come up here with Cait to fix it up.

"Look, Cait. It's your little buddy," Henry said as he waved to June and Blake. Blake was taking a few sticks of sidewalk chalk to his driveway while his mother sipped on an iced tea.

June waved as Henry and Cait pulled up into their driveway next door.

"Cait!" Blake dropped the chalk and ran up to the side of the car as Cait undid her seatbelt.

"Hey, Blake! How's it going, buddy?" Henry asked as he got out of the car. He laughed as the little boy held up his hand for a high five.

"All right!" Henry said as he high fived the tiny hand.

"Hey, Cait. You thirsty, honey?" June waved over as her son's friend got out of the car, running her hands through her long black hair.

"No thank you, Mrs. Hawkley," Cait replied. She gave a small smile as June walked over to greet them.

"Did you two have a nice drive up?" she asked.

"It was beautiful. It's so nice to be back," Henry replied. He ran his hands through his hair and smiled at the small house. In the back of his car were four cans of paint. He hoped to get the trim and garage door done in the next few days.

"Wow, Cait!" June exclaimed. "You certainly grew a lot this year, didn't you?"

"Just over six inches," Cait answered. "I was hoping for another inch or two. Then I would be as tall as Blake. I guess I'll have to wait another year."

"Oh, you. Always so serious," June said with a laugh. She winked up at Henry before telling her son to pick up his sidewalk chalk before the breeze got any stronger. "You two want to come over for dinner tonight?"

"What do you think, Cait?" Henry asked his daughter.

"Thank you very much for the offer," Cait said as she looked down to straighten the bottoms of her jeans, revealing a bare inch of shin above her socks. "These are too short, daddy."

"Well, we can go to the store later," Henry said. "I guess you grew more than I thought you did." He shrugged before opening the garage door.

"Well, bring your appetites. I'm making lasagna." June waved before she trotted back over to her yard.

"Cait, why don't you bring your bag into the house before you two run off and find trouble," Henry suggested.

"I don't get into trouble, daddy," Cait responded. She handed Blake the small cloth bag and asked him to hold it up. Henry chucked as his little girl dropped her book collection back into it.

"Anything new around town, Blake?" Henry asked.

"There's a new restaurant down there," Blake replied, pointing down the road. "Mom said she wants to go check it out."

"That sounds good," Henry said. "Alright, Cait, once you've put your stuff together, you two can run along and go play. Just don't go too far, okay? Don't go near the beach without asking, and be careful around the road, okay?"

"Yes, daddy," Cait said.

"Okay," Blake answered.

Saturday – 6:00 p.m.

June poured Henry a glass of red wine, pausing afterwards to smile at the children as they played on the floor next to the dining room. Blake had run after dinner to show Cait his new chess and checkerboard, asking her to teach him how to play.

"You know how to play chess already, honey?" June asked as she sat down back down at the table.

"Yes Mrs. Hawkley. Daddy taught me how a few months ago."

"Well, that's just amazing," June said with a wink to Henry. "And it's just Ms. Hawkley now."

"Ted finally signed the papers?" Henry asked, lowering his voice a bit.

"He did, yes," June replied. "It's for the best. He sees Blake every other weekend, and I get to retain my sanity." She sipped her wine. "What about you? How'd it pan out with that girl you brought up here last summer?"

"Oh, about as well as the rest," Henry admitted with a shrug. "My job at the university keeps me so busy. It feels like I barely have time for Cait, let alone anyone else. That's why I love coming up here so much during the summer. It's the most I get to see her all year."

He looked over to see his daughter explain the different movements a knight could make on the chess board. Blake nodded and tried it out for himself.

"You guys want some dessert?" June asked. "I have some chocolate cake on the counter I made this morning."

"Yeah!" Blake shouted as he got up.

Cait stood up and straightened her clothing before walking over and saying, "Yes, please."

"Oh my gosh, she gets politer each year," June said. "Blake, honey, you know where the plates are. Help Cait out, okay?"

"Okay, mom," Blake said.

Turning back to Henry, June said, "It's a shame if you ask me."

"Hmm?" Henry asked.

"You not settling down."

"Oh, hell. I've already been down that path," Henry answered.

"I know, but, well if you don't mind me saying," June began, "Cait's such a bright girl, but she's still a little girl, and little girls need attention."

"Well, I may work a lot, but I'm still there for her every day," Henry said. His posture stiffened a tad in response.

"Oh no, don't misunderstand," June said, touching Henry's arm. "I'm sorry, I just meant... well... she's so serious. She could use a good female role model in her life, is all I wanted to say."

Henry turned away from June to look at Cait again, who was sitting up straight on June's couch with her cake. She held her plastic fork carefully so as not to get any chocolate on her face. It was a concern that Blake did not share.

"Oh, it's okay, June," Henry sighed. "I'm trying with her. It's just, after her mom passed away, I never got the urge to date seriously again." He sipped his wine again. "Seven years ago, this summer."

"Cait was just a baby," June said.

"Yes, she was."

"I'm sorry," June said as she reached up to rub Henry's shoulder. "It's not my place. I just care about you both. It's hard not to." She leaned over to whisper. "Blake was so excited when I told him you two were coming up again. He hasn't talked about anything else for a week. It's adorable how inseparable they become each summer."

"It is. And don't worry about it. I didn't take offense. Besides, you're probably right. Even the guys in the lab remark on how much like a little scientist she sounds."

"Well, we can talk about it later. For right now, there's this new restaurant in town my son is dying to see. I say the four of us go there tomorrow night," June said, smiling back over at the kids.

"Tomorrow?" Henry asked. "Well, I wouldn't want to impose."

"Oh no, mister," June said, poking him in the arm. "We're going to make sure you have fun while you're up here!"

Sunday – 2:10 p.m.

Henry took off his sunglasses as he pulled his car into the driveway. His backseat was filled with supplies from the hardware store in town. He smiled as he thought about little Cait helping him paint the trim in the basement.

He stepped out of the car and walked out of the garage, taking in the beautiful view. Across the street there was a small cliff that made its way down to the beach. He and June had agreed to take the kids surf fishing before they headed out to dinner.

"Cait?" Henry called out. He walked around the garage to the backyard. "You here?"

There was no answer. He shrugged, assuming the kids were probably up to no good somewhere. They had already been playing together when he left right before 1:00.

Henry walked over to the small patch of grass between the houses.

"Blake? Cait?" He continued to move back towards the driveways. "June?"

The windows on June's house were closed, the curtains were drawn, and the lights were turned off. Her car was parked in its usual spot. He thought it odd the house that normally teemed with the most life on the street be so eerily silent.

"Cait?" Henry called out louder.

His head turned around as he heard a faint cry. He took a step towards the street, calling out to his daughter again. Again, there was a faint cry. Henry's feet began to move faster.

"Daddy?"

It was a muffled, soft cry for help. Henry ran across the street, dodging a car that came around the curve. He looked over the ledge to see the small, tattered clothing covering his daughter's body.

"Cait!" Henry yelled.

"Daddy..." Cait mumbled between coughs. There was a small trickle of dried blood that had dripped from her face onto the large, flat rock.

"I'm coming! Just stay right there!" Henry yelled again as he grabbed onto the edge and lowered himself down. He landed on the rock next to Cait. Leaning over, the panicked father reached down and cradled his little girl in his arms.

Cait's arms hung limp. She was breathing, but it was shallow and infrequent. Her cheeks were soaked with a mixture of tears and blood. She coughed again, depositing a few small specks of blood onto her father's shirt.

"Hold on. Just hold on!" Henry held her as he stepped down onto the path. He ran as fast as he could without jostling her too much. Eventually, he rounded the curb and came back onto the street. Cait reached up with one her hands and touched his face.

"It hurts," she mumbled.

"I know, baby, I know. Let's get you inside. I'm gonna help you." He stepped back onto the street, looking both ways before he started walking.

As he crossed the center line, a pair of eyes caught his. He could see Blake's young face staring at him through a window. The boy had been crying; his hand was pressed up against the glass.

June came up and stood behind her son. Henry called out to her and asked for help. His heart sank as the cold, distant look on her face registered. His friend and neighbor of years slowly backed away from the window. She pulled Blake back as well before allowing the curtain to close.

Henry slowly looked down at Cait's face. The wind had blown her hair aside, showing a deep cut on her temple and cheek. The cut was just large enough to reveal a collection of circuitry where her brain should have been.

The distressed father slowly looked back up at June's house, putting two and two together. He fought a swell of emotion as he continued his stride across the street and up his driveway.

"Henry?"

The voice belonged to Martin Floyd, the old man in his seventies who lived on the other side of June's house. The old man trotted down his front steps and as fast as his legs could carry him. Henry could see the pins on the old veteran's hat glint in the sunlight.

"She okay?" Martin asked, taking off his hat.

"I don't know," Henry said as he hurried inside, leaving the old man behind.

"You need me to call someone?" Martin called out. The old veteran waved his bent arms to steady himself as he made his way through June's lawn.

"Help! Help! We need help!" Martin yelled. He reached up and knocked on June's front door. "Miss Hawkley! Help!" He did it's best to project his old, craggy voice. After a moment of silence, Martin knocked again.

"Miss Hawkley?"

"Go away, Martin," June's voice replied.

"It's Cait, Miss Hawkley!" Martin pleaded. "The little girl is hurt! Henry took her inside."

"It's not a little girl," June answered.

"What do you mean?"

"Abomination," June said, her voice thick with distaste. "Go. Look at her. Look at her head."

"All I saw was a hurt little girl and her daddy," Martin said before stepping back and walking down her steps. The elderly neighbor made his way over to Henry's house as fast as he could.

Sunday - 3:20 p.m.

Martin Floyd stood behind Henry and stared at the young, scholarly father who was frantically trying his best to tend to his daughter's wound. The girl had remained unconscious since Henry carried her inside over an hour ago.

The old man offered to call for an ambulance several times after following Henry inside. Each time, Henry had politely but firmly said no, saying that there was nothing they could do.

Instead of leaving, Martin stayed. He fetched towels, water, and some tools from a shelf in the garage. The lines in his face sunk with despair as he watched the frantic father try again and again to revive his daughter. When he failed, he began to tend to the massive wound on her temple.

The impact had cracked her skull open. After a half an hour, Martin worked up the nerve to lean over and peek at the wound.

Inside the gash was a mix of shiny metal, tiny lights, and circuitry. June was right. For a moment, it filled him with terror. He swallowed hard, turned around, and ran out the door.

Before he could follow through with his instinct to flee, he saw a tear streak down Henry's face as the distraught father turned to watch him go. It dropped off his face, landing onto the tattered shirt of little Cait. It broke the old man's heart to see.

After that, Martin made the decision to stay. No matter what it was in her head, he could not see anything more than an injured little girl and a father trying his best to keep her alive.

A shuddered sigh from Henry interrupted Martin's train of thought.

"Cait... Cait it's me," Henry whispered. "I'm here."

"Daddy?" Cait asked. The girl tried to roll her eyes down to look at her father. She reached up and grabbed her two of his fingers with her small, bruised hands.

"I'm here, Cait," Henry whispered.

"I'm cold," Cait mumbled.

Henry looked over to Martin, who reached down and picked up a small blanket from one of the chairs in the living room. The two men tucked it around Cait's limp body.

"Thank you," she said.

"Do you know how long you were down there? What time did you fall?" Henry asked her.

"It was around 1:00. We were playing. I tried to catch the ball. Blake rolled it to me," Cait asked before coughing, which brought winces of pain. "I tried to catch it... but I slipped."

"It was an accident," Henry soothed.

"I'm sorry..." Cait said before closing her eyes again. She continued to move her little torso up and down. Henry took out a small electronic tool and held it up to her forehead for a minute before looking back at Martin.

"Cait and her mother were in a car crash when she was just seven months old. The car skidded on ice, plowing through a guardrail and going over the edge," Henry explained. His voice was soft with the air of defeat. "Susan was killed in the crash, but Cait clung to life in the hospital ICU."

"I'm so sorry," Martin replied.

"After two weeks, the doctors told me she would probably never wake up. There was too much brain damage." Henry wiped away a tear as he recalled the account to his older neighbor. "I asked that I be allowed to take her home, to die with her family."

"They let you?"

"They did," Henry answered. "I took her to my lab instead. I knew that if I could get there in time..."

He trailed off as he reached down to stroke his daughter's hair.

"What kind of work do you do at the university?" Martin asked.

After a long sigh, Henry said, "I've been studying artificial intelligence. Learning computers. I also tinker with robotics."

"Oh my," Martin exclaimed. "That thing in her head?" he asked, pointing to the wound.

"Her brain could never have repaired itself, but I could give her a chance to grow, to live! I replaced the damaged hemisphere with an artificial learning machine," Henry explained. "It took me nearly forty hours to get it right." He reached over and picked up a glass of water to soothe his dry, exhausted voice. "A few days after the procedure, she opened her eyes. She smiled at me and cooed, like she always did."

"It worked?"

"It worked!" Henry smiled softly as he looked back at Martin once again. "I knew that... I knew it would change who she was. And, it was difficult for her at first. She had to learn all over again as the computer adapted. She had to relearn how to crawl, how to take a bottle, how to hold her toys..."

"She always seemed like a bright girl," Martin remarked.

"After a few weeks, her artificial intelligence began to adapt and work with what remained of her brain." Henry wiped tears away from his eyes before continuing. "I don't know if I can explain it in a way that will make sense, Martin. My wife was dead. My little girl was braindead." His head sunk down as his shoulders went limp. "I knew I could help her... I had to help her..."

"My little boy got hit by a car when he was nine," Martin said. "He was riding his bike. Dumb teenager behind the wheel didn't see him. I stayed at the hospital with him night and day, not knowing if he was going to recover."

"Did he?" Henry asked.

"Eventually, yeah," Martin responded. "He woke up after a few days. Took him a while, but he healed up."

"I'm glad he was okay," Henry whispered as he stared into space.

"Point is, for those few days, there wasn't anything I wouldn't have done for my boy," Martin explained.

"Thank you."

"Be right back," Martin said before standing up from his chair. He turned and made his way out the front door. Sighing after he stepped off Martin's porch, the kind neighbor took a package of cigarettes out of his pocket. He removed one from the pack and pulled the tab, sparking the front of it.

They did not have the kick of the ones from his youth, but nowadays they were the only option. Synthetic tobacco was kinder to the lungs, or so the manufacturers label said.

"He didn't call the ambulance, did he?"

Martin turned to see June; her face a mask of cold detachment. Like his earlier exchange with her through her front door, it threw him for a loop. She was normally one of the most pleasant and warm people in the neighborhood.

"No. Said there was nothing they could do," Martin replied.

"Heh," June snorted derisively. "It's more likely he was worried they'd take his little science experiment away." She stared straight ahead, looking off past the part of the street where Cait had tumbled down earlier in the day.

"It's a little girl, June," Martin said. He tried his best to hide his growing disgust for a person who had been his neighbor for ten years.

"It's not a girl. It's not a child. It's not even human!" June snapped, raising her voice. "My son has been friends with that... thing, for years. They write letters to each other, play together. Who knows what he's gotten from her."

Martin stared at the mother as she raised a glass to her lips with trembling hands. While her voice gave off the impression that she was calm and measured, the rest of her looked like an angry, nervous wreck.

"I've seen your kids play for years, June. Seems to me all they got from each other was friendship."

"You can't be friends with something that isn't alive," June retorted.

"Well maybe you don't know what the hell you're talking about!" Martin glowered.

"Excuse me?"

"I said you don't know what the hell you're talking about," Martin repeated. "It's real rich, you judging without knowing the whole story."

"I saw the stuff in her head. I know what Henry does at his lab. I've seen all I need to know. That thing in there is a God damned abomination!"

"That thing in there is the same little girl that his wife gave birth to," Martin corrected.

"What?"

"I said it's his daughter." The old man coughed between puffs of his cigarette. "She was in the same accident that killed his wife. He kept her alive when nothing else could."

June paused and stood in silence. She held her glass at waist level, turning to look at the older neighbor out of the corner of her eye.

"So, she's got some artificial parts in her head, so what? She still got all the stuff that makes her who she is." Martin flicked his cigarette onto the driveway and stepped on it. "I don't care what you think, but that's your little boy's best friend in there."

Turning back towards the porch, Martin said, "You ought to be ashamed of yourself. Decades ago, it was people like you who would've kept someone like me from playing with my white friends when I was a kid."

"That is completely different."

"I don't see how it is," Martin scoffed before walking back up the stairs to Henry's front door.

June took another sip of wine as Henry's front door closed. She could feel her son's eyes burning into the back of her head as she stood on her lawn. He had not stopped asking to see Cait since she dragged him inside hours ago.

AROUND THE DARK DIAL

Sunday – 8:49 p.m.

Henry sat in his favorite easy chair. He leaned forward, cradling Cait in his arms and humming the melody to one of Cait's favorite songs. Martin had fallen asleep in another chair on the other side of the room as the light through the windows had faded away with the sunset.

The work to save little Cait had stopped an hour ago. Henry's fingers were now sore from handling the tiny tools. One part of the artificial half of her brain would stop functioning. After he reconnected it, another would fail. The circuits that connected the artificial intelligence to the other half of her brain, spinal cord, and nervous system refused to keep working for more than a few minutes at a time.

Henry's hands, covered with dried blood and soldering flux, trembled as he cradled his daughter's limp body. The only movement from her was the gentle rise and fall of her chest as she took shallow breaths.

"Daddy?"

Henry's heavy eyelids snapped open, and he looked down at his girl's face. Her eyes were heavy, but open.

"I'm here, Cait."

"I'm tired," she breathed.

"I know. It's okay."

"I'm sorry, daddy. Sorry I fell. Sorry I…"

"Sorry what, Cait? What is it?"

"Sorry I scared Miss Hawkley."

"What do you mean?"

"She found me," Cait recalled. "I was down there. She picked me up. I got tired. When I opened my eyes, she was gone."

Henry's face burned. He wanted to scream in rage but tried his best to keep his composure. He looked over and recognized a similar simmering expression on Martin's face, who had woken up a few moments ago.

"It's okay, Cait."

"Is Blake okay?" Cait asked.

"He's fine. He's gonna be just fine, baby," Henry reassured.

"I scared her, didn't I?" Cait asked her father.

"What?"

"She saw me. She left me there..." Cait cried. Her eyes closed tightly, forcing tears down the side of her face.

Henry used to fear that the technology he used to replace the damaged part of her brain would never allow her to experience the full range of emotions that makes someone who they are. The tears falling down her cheek were not in response to pain receptors firing. They were flowing freely as she tightened her grip on her father's shirt.

She was upset. Crying. Afraid.

"I thought she was my friend," Cait cried out softly.

"It's okay, everything's going to be fine," Henry hugged the little girl to his body.

"Daddy..."

"I'm here."

"I'm sorry I can't help you with our house..."

Now it was Henry's turn to cry. His tears landed on his shirt, his arm, and Cait's near-motionless chest. He realized she was not only in pain, but aware of her prognosis.

She knew she was dying. And despite his two PhD's and years of experience, there was nothing he could do to help her.

It was one of the reasons he was often so strict, and worried whenever she would play outside. Half of her brain may have been artificial, but it was just as vulnerable to injury as the rest of her.

"I'm so sorry, Cait. I'm so sorry I wasn't there for you," Henry whispered, fighting back the urge to burst out crying. "I'm supposed to protect you. To keep you safe. And I didn't do it. I'm so, so sorry..."

"It's okay." Cait reached up and grabbed her dad's arm with her hand. "I... I remember..."

"What do you remember, baby?"

"I remember what you did for me... Helped me. Thank you." She breathed deeply. "I love you, daddy."

Henry's dam broke. His body shuddered as he sobbed, holding his girl to his chest. It was the first time she had ever said that to him. For years he wondered and worried she might never have the capability to understand those kinds of emotions.

"I love you too..."

Henry's bawling continued as his daughter's hands eventually loosened their grip and fell to her sides. He held his breath, his eyes wide in disbelief and shock, as the small lights coming from the machinery visible through the wound in her head went out.

Martin took off his hat and lowered his head, unable to fight back tears as they rolled down his cheeks. He watched the broken father stand up, still cradling his little girl in his hands. The old vet put both of his hands over his mouth as he watched his neighbor carrying his daughter back over to the table where he had worked on her and place her down.

Henry reached down and kissed Cait on the forehead before using his hand to close her eyes. Eventually, he grabbed a blanket and placed it over the small, lifeless body. After she was covered, the dad collapsed under his own weight next to the table, sobbing uncontrollably.

The minutes ticked by as Henry laid next to the table. The world around him faded away as his eyes blurred with tears and his own crying drowned out other sounds.

He remained unaware as Martin walked over to the front door. Henry had asked him to keep the old wooden door open so that the gentle breeze could flow through the screen door, claiming that Cait loved the smell of the ocean air on the breeze.

Henry failed to notice that June had stepped up to the screen door just before Cait had mustered up the strength to say goodbye. His neighbor's cold, calloused expression had eroded to be replaced by one of utter anguish.

AROUND THE DARK DIAL

Henry continued to weep for his daughter as Martin closed the wooden door in June's face.

J.D. SANDERSON

HELLO AGAIN

One-by-one, each of the creature's three legs stepped out from behind the massive tree. Its head, if that is indeed what it was, bobbed from left to right and back again. The motion was almost bird-like.

Two bony limbs extended from what appeared to be a torso. Like the rest of its body, they were covered in a gray skin. This outer layer might have been a covering of tiny scales, but it was impossible to tell from this distance. The only place that varied in color was on the head where human eyes would be. But, instead of the expected orbs, the areas were simply black and seemed to sink into the surrounding skin like pools. No mouth or nose were present, at least not as humans understood them.

The creature stepped forward, clearing the surrounding trees. The gait was smooth and graceful, but unlike any land animal on Earth. After a moment of moving its head, supposedly looking up and down at the figure standing before it, the two-meter entity lifted one of its arms and spread the webbed digits at the end.

The fingers, for lack of a better term, moved in different directions. It was not random or chaotic, but thoughtful.

After several more gestures, the lifeform crouched, bending its three legs at the knees. The legs straightened as it shot into the air. It flew overhead, disappearing into the glare of the sun. Wherever it went from there was anybody's guess.

That was the tale told not by some digital recording, but by two dozen photographs and one eyewitness.

Gerren Weber and Major Prisha Patel sat in silence as three people on the other side of the large conference table looked over the pictures from Gerren's antique camera. It was the third meeting on the encounter that Major Patel had been to over the past few weeks, and the first Gerren had been allowed to attend.

Five weeks ago, Gerren had been one of the most accomplished expeditionary officers in the service. He resigned his commission after his encounter in what used to be Yellowstone Park, and had been pondering the possibility of civilian contract service when Prisha informed him — in a roundabout way — that he had not lost his mind.

She had taken the liberty of making copies of the photographs before sending the originals to Gerren. The top military minds scanned and catalogued them, saving the images for study. Top advisors assembled a team to analyze the lifeform in greater detail, and — if possible — establish contact.

One of those goals would be much harder than the other. Three more teams had entered the field since the first expedition by Gerren. None of them reported anything resembling a non-humanoid creature standing nearly two meters tall.

The three people across the table organized papers, data pages, and their own personal copies of Gerren's photographs.

"Shall we proceed?" Prisha said to the group. She had little patience for people who took their time starting meetings, being used to the promptness of the military. Civilian scientists, at least in her experience, were far too preoccupied with their work to ever be on time.

"Yes, sorry," Dr. Hadley Berringer replied. Hadley was one of the foremost biologists on the planet. Assumed to be the toughest get of the lot, she immediately cancelled her classes at Cambridge after looking at the now-classified entity. She shuffled the data in front of her one last time before continuing, "Okay, there we go. I just get so excited with the possibility of running into our friend there I get a bit carried away with the preparations."

"We all feel the same way," Dr. Joseph Onacona replied as he rifled through his own stack of papers. Joseph was one of the most requested linguists in the world. Like Gerren, he had been born to deaf parents and was fluent in sign language.

"And you, Ambassador?" Prisha asked.

Ambassador Daved Whittaker looked up from his coffee and nodded. Privately, Prisha found it quite amusing that one of the most respected diplomats in the world was also one of the quietest people she had ever met.

"I am," he answered.

"Glad to see there's an extra chair," someone said from behind Prisha and Gerren. Prisha cursed under her breath, recognizing it immediately.

Special Agent Samia Amel grabbed the seat next to Prisha. She leaned across the table to offer her hand to the other three people.

"Welcome to the party," Prisha said as she glared sideways at Samia. "I must admit, I wasn't aware you had been assigned to the team."

"The President agreed with us that someone from Intelligence should be included in any effort to contact the entity," Samia replied. "I'm delighted for the opportunity to join you all."

Prisha did her best to stifle an eyeroll. Despite not having run into her for nearly three years, she still found Samia's smooth manner of conversing was as grating and calculated as her look. The slicked back hair and stylish suit never failed to get on the Major's nerves. It was an opinion she had held since the two first met nearly twenty years ago at university.

During the past two weeks, Prisha repeatedly raised objections about including anyone from Intelligence during a first contact mission. She felt it unfortunate that she had to wait until now to find out that she lost the argument.

"Have you met Gerren Weber?" Prisha asked.

"The photographer? I have not. It's nice to meet you." Samia reached out and shook Gerren's hand.

"Well, let's get going, shall we?" Prisha said, trying again to get the meeting underway. "Since our physics expert is delayed and won't be here for a while yet, would you like to kick us off, Dr. Berringer?"

"Oh, yes. Absolutely," Hadley said as she fiddled with her data pads. "I've been looking over the images of the lifeform. The implied evolutionary path is unlike anything seen on Earth." The Cambridge biologist smiled as she looked down again at the images.

"Go to school a long time, Doctor?" Samia asked.

Hadley's expression changed from excitement to confusion as she looked over to the intelligence agent. "I, um... I was just about to remark what an extraordinary discovery that Gerren here made."

"Your job in this is to use your considerable expertise into evolutionary biology to determine what this thing is, and what kind of threat it may pose to us," Samia said.

"Now, wait a minute," Prisha interjected, "we have no reason to believe the creature is a threat to us."

"You're suggesting we kid-glove a lifeform that happened to appear in the middle of the field during our first expedition? A field that, may I remind you, mysteriously appeared during one of the most devastating natural disasters in our history. How do we know this entity, or others like it, are not responsible for those events?"

"Samia..." Prisha growled.

"And, lastly," Samia continued, "that this thing managed to somehow camouflage itself against the most sensitive surveillance equipment in the world?"

"It didn't evade detection completely," Daved remarked.

"Because it obviously was not planning for something as primitive as a film camera," Samia retorted. "Mr. Weber was extremely lucky to have been in the right place at the right time with his... *antique.*"

"I saw it with my eyes before I saw it through the lens," Gerren added.

"The fact that it evaded electronic detection does not mean it's inherently hostile," Daved said.

"Oh?" Samia asked, leaning forward.

"It may have generated some kind of interference, or it could be a natural phenomenon related to its biology." Hadley looked down at her papers as she spoke, careful to evade Samia's piercing stare.

"Until you can bring me sufficient evidence that proves it did not intend to hide itself from our technology, I am forced to assume the worst," Samia said as she leaned back in her chair and pressed her fingertips together in an arch.

"We won't know anything until we try and talk to it."

Everyone turned to look at Joseph, who was accessing the main monitor at the head of the room. He turned on the display, revealing enhanced scans of three of the photographs.

"You and Gerren both believe it uses some sort of sign language to communicate," Prisha relayed to the rest of the group, trying her move things along from Samia's verbal barrage.

"Yes," Joseph answered. "I agree with Mr. Weber. The pictures he took of the alien's hand movements seem to be consistent with our understanding of gestural language."

"That, and the fact it has no mouth," Hadley giggled. Her smile quickly faded after catching another cold look from Samia.

"Alright. Enough. What kind of security measures have you taken to keep this thing in the field, and keep people out?" Samia interjected. "You were planning on doing that, weren't you?"

"With the barrier continuing to fade, we've been relying more on troops to secure the perimeter," Prisha said. "Five people were arrested last two days attempting to cross the barrier."

"If any of them had gotten inside and seen the creature..." Gerren pondered.

"We'd have a panic on our hands," Daved concluded.

Standing up, Samia said, "I want recommendations on my desk tomorrow morning by 9:00 a.m. Intelligence is going to be taking over the offices in the forward operating base near the field."

"My base?" Prisha asked, turning her head slowly towards her old college classmate.

"Yes. Here are the transfer orders." Samia placed a pad in front of Prisha. "Don't worry, your office will still be there."

Samia turned and exited the room, allowing the door to slam shut behind her.

"That went well," Gerren muttered.

*   *   *

"Hello, Samia," Gerren said as he turned into the mess hall. He had felt the animosity between Samia and Prisha whenever they were within a hundred feet of one another. Still, he decided that was no reason not to be polite. "Getting a bite to eat before bed?"

"Just a drink of water," she said. "I believe your friend the Major forgot to order someone to stock up my room."

"I always like to fill up the night before a mission," Gerren laughed. "Usually the morning of I'm too nervous to eat very much."

"I understand," Samia replied. She picked up a second bottle of water before turning to look at Gerren. "You must be looking forward to this. Must be quite rewarding for you?"

"Rewarding?"

"Well, it does prove you didn't suffer a psychological

break, right?"

"I suppose so," Gerren said through a forced smile.

"Tell me," Samia continued, "how fast was the creature?"

"How fast?"

"Do you think it could it outrun a human?" she asked.

"Well, I don't know," Gerren said. "I didn't really see it run. It just kind of, jumped."

"Yes, I know. I read your report. I am asking you to give me your opinion. If it's not too much trouble."

"Honestly, I'm not sure," he said. His shoulders tensed up. The look on her face could have melted glass.

"What about weapons?" Samia asked.

"It wasn't wearing anything, if that's what you're asking."

"And yet it evaded your helmet cam and jumped out of sight. Nice to see your powers of observation are so...astute."

Samia turned and walked back to her cabin, leaving Gerren flushed and anxious.

Gerren dropped his snack on his nightstand after closing the door to his cabin. His fingers fidgeted on the edge of his bunk, wrestling with a swirl of anticipation, anxiety, and fear now coursing through his formerly relaxed nerves. In eight hours, the team would step through the barricade and enter the field, hoping to find whatever the hell that thing was. Now he knew Samia was not going into the field tomorrow to make first contact. She was going to pick a fight.

He laid down on the bed, hoping that the sounds of people moving around out in the hallway would provide enough white noise to lull him to sleep. After a few minutes, a faint sound caused his eyes to snap open.

Gerren sat up to see a small piece of paper on the floor that someone evidently slid under the crack in his doorway. He sprang up from his cot and picked it up, unfolding it before he sat back down.

Inside were just two words:

"Be Ready"

* * *

Ambassador Daved Whittaker watched Major Patel and Gerren strap on their protective equipment, following along as close as possible with his own. Next to him was Hadley, Joseph, and Dr. Jakob Miles, a physicist who had been filling everyone's ears for nearly fifty minutes with a myriad of possible transportation methods the lifeform could have used to arrive in the field. Even Samia had given up trying to bully him into silence.

"Everyone ready?" Prisha asked the group.

"Yes," replied Hadley.

"Why do we need the helmets?" Daved asked.

"Because we're going to make contact with an alien?" Prisha smirked.

"Well, we don't know it is an alien, necessarily," Jakob chimed. "It could be an alien, or it could be something from below the surface—"

"Let's get going," Samia interrupted. "Helmets on. Visors down."

The team closed the transparent carbon fiber shields. Several clicks rang out as they locked into place automatically. Daved, Jakob, and Hadley all visibly relaxed as the oxygen began to pump in.

Gerren looked over to see Samia reach down and pick up a pulse rifle. He may not have been up to snuff with the latest models, but he knew enough to tell it had both an enhanced power cell and sights.

"Are you sure that's a good idea?" Gerren asked.

Samia replied with a long stare.

"We're going in to make contact, aren't we?" Jakob asked. "I didn't think we were going in to kill it."

"Let's move out," Samia ordered and walked to the hatch with the rifle across her chest, at the ready, as if that was all the answer she needed to give to their questions.

The seven of them exited the back of the base through the hatch. The crowds had lessened over the past few weeks, and Prisha had instructed her troops to extend an opaque cylindrical walkway tunnel to the edge of the field. The last thing she or Samia wanted was for the civilian team members to be overwhelmed more than necessary.

The green tinted field was twice as transparent as it was during the initial expedition by Gerren weeks ago, and the top scientists in the world had no clue why.

The group wandered through a clearing past a

cluster of blue-green trees. Hadley grabbed Gerren's arm, halting him in his tracks. She pointed down to the ground, where he saw a small mammal running across the grass in front of them. It was about the size of a chipmunk, sported red and yellow fur, and had enormous black eyes compared to its little head.

Gerren smiled down at the creature that he initially spotted during his first run. They were everywhere inside the field. Prisha pointed up towards one of the trees ahead at a large bird. It was the size of an American Eagle, but had a straighter beak, larger talons, and green and blue feathers.

The trio picked up the pace to catch up with everyone else. Prisha gave the signal to spread out.

"Ten meters apart," Prisha said. "Keep your scanners on. I don't expect we'll see much on them, if anything, but we don't want to leave any stone unturned."

"Agreed," Samia added.

"I'm surprised the grass is so low," Daved commented.

"Field Deer," Prisha replied. "About the size of a water buffalo. You can't miss them."

"Docile?" Joseph asked.

"Afraid of everything," Gerren said. "Fast as hell, too."

"What about predators?" Daved asked.

"Field Zone Wolves," Gerren replied, holding up his hand knee high. "Smaller than a gray wolf, but with bigger teeth. Faster too. Gray fur with a bluish streak down the back."

"Didn't you read the briefing packet, Ambassador?" Hadley inquired.

"I was busy preparing. I like to meditate a bit before a negotiation or conference," Daved explained.

"I'm glad you were able to find time to review the materials, Hadley," Samia muttered. Daved looked straight ahead as he walked, choosing instead not to respond to her remark.

The group walked for several hours, stopping to rest three times throughout the afternoon. A short while ago, Gerren had led the team past the trees where he first encountered the lifeform. Their scans had, unsurprisingly, revealed nothing out of the ordinary.

Prisha waved her arm to draw the rest of the team in.

"The sun is setting. This looks like as good a spot as any to set up camp."

"Sounds good to me," Joseph said, dropping his pack.

"Me too," said Daved. Hadley nodded in agreement.

"Fine," Samia said. They were in the middle of a clearing with the nearest trees fifty yards away. It would be hard to sneak up on them with nothing to provide cover.

Samia dropped her pack and pulled out a collapsible tent. She unfolded the shelter and locked it into place. The rest of them followed suit.

"Anyone hungry?" Prisha asked.

* * *

Light wisps of smoke rose from the fire for several minutes after the embers finally gave out their red glow. One-by-one, the team retreated to their tents, excited and nervous about what tomorrow could bring.

The team had decided to head deeper into the Field zone. Additional survey teams and mapping drones had uncovered dozens of locations of interest within several hours walk.

Gerren crawled outside, careful not to step on anything brittle or cause a disturbance. He zipped up the door of his tent, hoping nobody would notice he was gone. There was no way to know whether someone would awake before he returned. Nevertheless, he made sure to take every precaution he could.

He switched on his wrist light after stepping over the laser perimeter. Samia and Prisha had set it up thirty meters out in all directions. Gerren was confident that his light would not awake someone from this distance.

As Gerren walked under the night sky, the sky was full of stars, clearer than he ever remembered seeing it. It was a gorgeous setting.

He eventually returned to the spot where he first raised his camera and snapped images of the three-legged creature. He stepped over roots near the humungous tree and walked around its trunk.

It was eerily quiet, with no insect or animal sounds to be heard. Only an occasional breeze cut through the silence. Gerren took several steps through a bed of moss and dirt towards another nearby tree, then a sound caught him by surprise.

He swore to himself with the realization that he forgot to lock in his helmet visor. He scrambled to lock it in as quickly as possible.

Three heavy footsteps hit the ground behind him. Gerren turned around as slowly as he could manage, hoping that he would not spook whatever it was. He said a quick prayer that a curious field deer had gotten too close.

The legs were the first things he saw. Three gray limbs — rigid, smooth and muscular — were partially obscured by a meter-high shrub. Gerren's looked up to see bony hips and a waist that dipped in sharply before leading up to a lean torso.

A pair of sack-like appendages hung off each side of the hips. There were small slits at the end of the organic bags. Whatever purpose they served eluded Gerren completely.

Its hands hung at its sides, and its head bobbed from side to side like a confused bird.

Gerren kept his light down. He worried that he might spook it if he aimed his flashlight in its face. Even aiming it towards the thing's legs, there was more than enough illumination to get a good luck.

He was much closer to it this time. During the first expedition, he had been a dozen meters away or more. Now, there was less than two meters that separated them.

The creature raised a slender gray arm to waist level.

The nine webbed fingers spread out before moving and taking shape.

The fingers bent and curled. As before, the movements were conscious and purposeful.

Gerren took off the wrist light and secured it to his shoulder, so that it pointed up. Raising his hands, Gerren decided to play a hunch.

"Hello again," he signed. He stared at the creature's head. The deep, black eye-like patches appeared to be fixated on his hands.

"My name is Gerren," he signed again. "Who are you? Where did you come from?" His hands were not as fast as they used to be, but he remembered all the signs he grew up using with his parents.

He didn't believe it would be able to understand him. His hope, rather, was that it would see they had something in common.

The gray figure stepped closer, its three legs moving in an incredibly graceful fashion. To Gerren's surprise, it held out a webbed hand. The creature stared him in the eye as it waited for him to make the next move.

* * *

Samia stepped around a group of smaller bushes. She walked toe-first, aiming one of her lights at the ground. The other light, mounted on top of her pulse rifle, illuminated the path ahead of her.

The intelligence agent had followed a set of tracks made by a men's size-nine boot for nearly a kilometer.

She knew Gerren was the only man with a size nine in the team.

Clearing another bush, Samia came to a clearing in front of the trees seen in Gerren's photographs. She continued to follow the tracks until the ended near a patch of moss. A few meters away were sets of prints she did not recognize. They were made by a heavy animal with three deep toe prints on two sides and what looked like the impression of a heel on another.

Samia knew the second set of tracks came from the creature. She also knew the tracks for both of them ended here. A quick lap around two trees revealed nothing. Her teeth locked in a frustrated grimace as she realized they had disappeared.

"Damn..."

J.D. SANDERSON

THE SNOWSTORM

    The long, punishing howl of snow and wind continued to push against the old, creaky windows of the tiny wooden cottage.
    What was originally forecasted to be a just a few inches of snow had swelled into one of the largest blizzards in decades. After three days, the deadly mixture of snow, drift, and high winds at last forced the cottage's lone resident to give up trying to keep her front walk clear every few hours.
    It simply wasn't worth the strain on her eighty-one-year-old body. Her only hope would be that her supply of food, water, and medicine would hold out until either

the temperature rose or officials from the government could come by and dig her out.

The old woman stood up and walked to her window. A deep breath rattled out of her as she pulled the heavy curtain aside to check on the drift. She guessed there was now over two feet of snow covering the walkway leading to her door. The whistling of the teapot snapped her out of her woeful gazing.

She poured the hot water inside her favorite mug, sniffing the air as the aroma of the tea began to spread. The elderly woman waited until the water had darkened sufficiently before removing the tea bag.

The strong herbal tea soothed her throat, which had felt raspier than normal after days of dry, freezing air blowing all over. She closed her eyes and listened to the crackling of the fireplace as she swallowed another sip.

They opened a minute later. She leaned forward, unsure if she was hearing things correctly. For an instant, it sounded like a voice was howling along with the wind.

She stood up, made her way to the window, and pulled the curtains aside. There was no sign of anyone. Just before she let go of the thick curtains, she spotted what looked like fresh tracks in the snow.

They led up the path to her door. Her front porch was not visible from this angle, but she knew tracks when she saw them.

Placing her tea on the coffee table, the woman scuttled over to the front door. She undid two deadbolts and the handle lock before turning the knob and pulling it open.

Through the screen door she saw a young man trudging up the walk to her house. He could not have been much older than twenty-five. In his arms was a bundle of cloth blankets. The stranger kept it close to his chest as he slogged through the snow drifts.

The bundle was crying.

The woman opened the screen door and motion for the man to come in.

"Hurry. Get inside!"

"Thank you," the young man coughed. "Thank you."

"Good lord," the woman exclaimed. "Don't have much sense, do you? Carrying a baby in this cold at three in the morning? Did you have a break down or something?"

"No," the man replied. "Well, yes. I mean, I got stuck in the drift, but I was trying to get here. I wanted to come see you. Your name is Mallory? Renae Mallory?"

"Why do you want to know?" The woman backed away, averting any direct eye contact from the man. "Are you alone?"

"Yes."

"Were you followed?"

"No..."

"You're sure?"

"Yes. Yes! Please. I wouldn't have come all this way if it wasn't important," he said. "I'm Dillan. This is my daughter, Isabel." The man peeled away a layer of blanket, revealing a flushed, exhausted looking baby girl underneath.

"She's adorable. Yes, I'm Renae. What do you want from me?"

"Well, I was told you can help people. Heal them," Dillan said.

"If your daughter has symptoms, it's too late. There's nothing more I can do," Renae stated.

"It's not her, it's my wife,"

"Your wife is sick?"

"Yes. She got the pox while she was out of town. She came back two days ago with a high fever," he explained. "This morning she woke up with the rash."

"Did she touch your daughter?" Renae asked.

"No, she's been in the garage since she came home. We didn't want to risk it."

"Good, good. May I see her?" Renae held out her arms.

Dillan removed the second blanket from baby Isabel before handing her to the old woman. He watched as his daughter stopped crying almost immediately after she looked up at the woman's weathered face.

"You have the gift," Dillan said. "It's why I had to come here. There were rumors of a healer up in an abandoned part of the old town near the hills."

"I'm not a healer," Renae responded as she looked down at the smiling baby.

"But people in town said you can prevent and heal disease!" Dillan protested. "My father even told me he heard of someone west of town who made little kids better. He used to tell me the stories when I was little." The young father wiped away a tear from his eye.

"When my wife got sick... I was desperate," he continued. "I knew I had to try to find you. I drove for two hours in the storm. My car got stuck in the drift. I bundled my girl up and walked until I saw the light from your house."

"You took a huge risk carrying her in the cold."

"I know. But I knew that if I took her home, she might die anyways. I need your help, please. If you can't help me, there's no hope. There's no other way to stop the plague."

"You know that by asking me for help you're breaking the law. Anyone suspected of having one of the plague diseases is supposed to go to one of the quarantine shelters until they are cleared," Renae said as she sat down. She lifted the baby's shirt to check for signs of infection.

"No sign of rash or fever. She's a healthy little girl," Renae confirmed. "You were right to isolate her from your wife." It was obvious immediately that her words took weight off the young man's shoulders.

"Thank you," Dillan breathed. "Will you help me?"

Renae stared at the young man, saying nothing.

"Please," Dillan pleaded, "I don't want her to get sick. The pox killed my little brother when I was a boy. Measles took my mother last winter." He wiped away a tear from his lower eyelid. "Can you help us?"

Renae let out a deep sigh before brushing her silver bangs out of her face. She waddled over to the front window again to peek outside. The snow was well on its way to filling up the tracks he left a few minutes ago. She let the curtains drop back into place as she turned around.

"How old is she?"

"She turns one next week."

"Give me a minute," she instructed. "Take off her pants."

"What?"

"I need to get to her legs. Take her pants off," Renae said. "I'll be with you in a moment."

The old woman shuffled her way through her kitchen towards a walk-in pantry. Once inside, she pulled a brown wooden box out of a small cabinet. She set the box down on the kitchen table, along with a worn, blue blanket.

"Bring her in here. I've got a spot for her on the kitchen table."

Dillan did as he was told. The baby cooed as she looked up at him from her new spot on the old wooden table.

"Can I do anything?" Dillan asked.

"Just hold her steady."

Renae pulled three slender tubes out of the box. It looked to Dillan as though they held water. There were sharp points on the ends.

"What are those things?" Dillan asked.

"Needles."

"You mean for sewing?"

"Not quite. These are for injecting."

Dillan reached down and plucked his daughter off the table. He backed away, cradling her against his chest.

"I thought you were a healer!" he yelled.

"I was a nurse before the convention," Renae said. "I can give your little girl something that will prevent her from getting sick."

"You mean a vaccination!"

"Yes."

"Jesus, God. You're insane! You're going to pump my daughter full of those things? They're poison! Everyone knows they get you sick or kill you outright. The lucky ones just end up slow."

"What did you think I was going to do? Wave my hands above her head, chant some ancient language, and bring down a light from the heavens to cleanse her?" Renae's voice dripped with sarcasm. It was a scenario she had lived out again and again over the decades. Unfortunately for any prospective patients, time had done little to help her understand what the past two generations had grown up believing.

"You've grown up believing something about medicine like this, so I'm sorry to throw cold water on you, but there is one way to prevent your daughter from getting one of the plagues — and that's to vaccinate her." Renae took a deep breath.

Dillan stared at her. He said nothing. He didn't need to. The shamed look in his eyes told her all she needed to know.

"I'm not trying to kill your daughter or contaminate your family. I'm trying to help."

"Maybe you're not a healer. Maybe I'll still find them," Dillan stammered.

"Go right ahead."

"It's against the law," Dillan said. "It's one of the most serious laws in the world."

"I'm not forcing you to do anything. I want to help you, but I'm not going to wait here in my kitchen all night."

"They can keep her from getting the pox?" Dillan stared down at the needles on the table, eventually glancing up at the baby in his arms.

"Pox, measles, mumps, yes. Polio, too," Renae confirmed. "If she doesn't get something from her mother, it'll be from someone else. Fifty million people die every year from the plagues, but you can give her a chance to live a long life. Today."

Calling them plagues left a bad taste in her mouth. At least three times a week during their regular broadcasts, the government made grandiose claims of progress in beating back ancient plagues with the latest mental and prayer techniques.

"Your stories from town are true in one respect," Renae admitted. "I'm not a healer, but I have helped prevent people from getting sick." She held up one of the needles. "I don't hurt children. I help then when I can."

Dillan relented, nodding and the setting his daughter back on the table.

"Can I hold her while you do it?"

"Of course." Renae examined one of the injections before removing the cap from the needle. "She's a beautiful girl. You're a lucky father."

"She's the spitting image of her mother," Dillan bragged.

"Make sure you hold her legs still," Renae instructed. "The needles can sting a bit, but she will be fine after it's all over. I promise you, her cries will not be an indication of something serious."

Dillan nodded, taking his daughters hand with one hand and her feet with the other. He leaned over and planted a kiss on her forehead

"What do they do?" he asked.

"This one is for smallpox. The others are for measles, mumps, and polio. They will make her immune to these plagues."

"And they work forever?"

"She will be safe, yes," Renae said with a nod. She adjusted her glasses before picking up the first needle.

Dillan leaned over to talk to his daughter as the crying began. His face curled inward, cringing as each of the needles entered his daughters small, chubby legs. The little girl's face turned beet red as she writhed and screamed. The infant's protesting continued as Renae applied four small bandages her legs.

"All done," Renae announced. "You can pick her up."

Dillan obliged, snatching the baby up and cradling her. He made funny faces and sounds, eventually drawing a giggle out of the child.

"I can help you too, if you like?" Renae held up a fresh needle.

"Me?"

"It's never too late," she said.

"I don't know," Dillan muttered. "They won't hurt a baby, since she had no say in the matter. But anyone seeking out or receiving a vaccine is sentenced to death."

"'For taking part in the voluntary spread of moral corruption, misinformation, and fear.' I know, I used to hear the same broadcasts." Renae scowled as she placed the needle back inside the box. "Well, let me know if you change your mind."

"You don't listen to the daily broadcasts anymore? But that's illegal."

"Oh, I know," Renae bristled. The remark caught Dillan by surprise. Even his father — who told him for years there were people with the power to prevent plagues, even though it was said to be impossible — never said something so blatantly harsh about The Leaders.

"But, The Leaders gave us the new laws. There hasn't been a war since the convention." Dillan shifted his daughter up, allowing her to rest her tired head on his shoulder.

"Do you remember before the convention?" Dillon asked her.

"Yes, I do," Renae admitted after a pause. "I was twenty-five. They were a small group for so long, until suddenly they weren't. They kept drumming up hysteria year after year. It creeped across the internet like a horde of termites until they had enough support to win an election."

"A what?"

"It was… it was how we selected leaders."

"But The Leaders are called upon," Dillan beamed. "The chosen receive the call to sit at one of the Seats of Shenton in the great Jenner Hall."

"Your father didn't tell you what it was like before the convention?"

"No. He was born ten years after."

Renae looked down to the sleeping baby in the young fathers' arms. She shuddered to think about what the world would be like when the child grew up.

At least she *would* grow up.

"Are you hungry?" Renae asked.

Dillan nodded, looking over to her kitchen counter. "Yes, ma'am."

"Why don't you go sit down on the couch. Let your little one get a bit more comfortable. I'll heat up a meal," Renae offered.

The eighty-one-year-old puttered around her kitchen, gathering a plate and some utensils. Her mind, still sharp after all these years, raced with the memories of the once-lauded global convention. The leaders of thirty countries met behind closed doors for two weeks, coming up with the new moral code.

It was the last big news event before the wave of official news broadcasters, corrected textbooks, and shaming booths for lawbreakers.

Fifty-six years. It had been fifty-six years since armed guards walked into her hospital and informed them they would no longer be poisoning children. Those like her were given the choice between resigning and finding other work or going to prison.

She remembered an older doctor, born at the end of the twentieth century, trying to explain to the soldiers how they were endangering the people they had sworn to protect. Minor cases of measles and chickenpox had been creeping across the coastal areas of the former United States for years.

He was the first person she saw gunned down as a "poisoner."

After the soldiers had left, Renae and a few of her friends snuck down to a locked storage room where they kept the newest vaccines. While more expensive than previous incarnations, they had a shelf-life of nearly one-hundred years.

She and her friends administered some whenever they could. A few a year was all they could risk without getting caught and sentenced to public shaming and death. Now she was running low.

"What's this?"

Renae turned back to see the young man staring at something near one of her bookshelves. Dillan had pulled a burgundy cloth off a circular object on a stand.

"That's a globe," she answered.

"A what?"

"It's a model of the Earth. Very old. It was my father's."

"Was this before they discovered the firmament? Before they knew how the planet really looked?"

"They talked about that long before it became against to law to mention otherwise," Renae uttered with disgust.

"Well, people are always making new discoveries," Dillan said. "It just took them a long time to break people of the lies the old governments kept spreading."

Renae shook her head in silence before taking the plate out of the warmer. She walked over and placed it on the coffee table, inviting the young man to sit down.

"Would you like me to hold her, so you can eat?" She offered.

"Oh, that's okay. I've gotten good at eating with one hand," Dillan whispered. He picked up a fork and had a bite of leftover chicken. "Thank you so much."

"You're welcome. You looked like you could use a meal." She watched Dillan finish off every morsel of the reheated meal. "What do you do for a living?"

"I work for the town," he answered, "distributing pamphlets and bulletins from The Leaders."

"Ah. A mail carrier," Renae said. "Must keep you busy."

"The Leaders always have good things for us to know." Dillan beamed with pride.

Renae walked over to the corner near her bookshelf. The beautiful, raised relief globe sat on a walnut stand. She still remembered asking her parents about all the different countries, and if they would ever have a chance to visit them. Now there were travel bans across most of the planet, set up to prevent the spread of the 'plagues.'

"Tell me, Dillan; do you know why they used to believe the Earth was round?" Renae continued to stare down at her father's globe as she waited for an answer.

"Because of the lies the government used to tell. They told us all about it in school."

"Oh, interesting. I'm curious. I haven't been to school in a long time. I graduated from college a few years before the convention." Renae sat in a chair next to the globe, dragging her fingertips along its surface as Dillan continued speaking about the information regularly spewed to the public.

"I think the storm is breaking," Dillan said. "Look!"

Renae stood up and walked to her front window. She could see the first few beautiful rays of sun peeking over the horizon. The snowstorm had stopped for the moment.

"It'll warm up soon. If I can get my car started, I can keep her warm enough to dig out the tire," Dillan speculated.

"You sure?" You're welcome to wait a few more hours if you wish. I might have some formula stocked somewhere."

"You've already done so much for my little girl and me. No matter what happens, I know she'll be okay."

"I vaccinated her against the major diseases in this part of the world," Renae clarified. "Travel to Asia, and you might be taking a risk. I wish I could have done more, but those were all I had left."

"How long have you been doing this?"

"Since it was illegal to do so."

Dillan's eyes widened as the gravity of the situation sunk in. He turned his head to stare again at the globe in the corner of her living room before looking back to his daughter. She was still sleeping in his arms.

"Thank you," he whispered.

"I helped you, young man. You can pay me back by helping me."

"What do you want me to do?" Dillan asked.

"Keep your mouth shut," Renae warned.

Dillan nodded. He tucked one of the blankets around his little girl's head before turning towards the door. Renae saw several beads of sweat around his temples. She could not tell if he was sweating from the anxiety of having broken a half dozen major laws, or because he had not taken off his heavy jacket all night.

The aging nurse reached and opened her front door. She held it open until she was sure he could make it past her driveway. The door closed after he reached a lower level of drift and could walk easier.

* * *

Renae sat at her television two days later, waiting for the midday broadcast to end. The smiling newscaster had just finished reading a story about a forthcoming expedition to the great ice barrier at the edges of the earth.

It took all her energy to avoid rolling her eyes as she sipped her tea. She was about to get up and make another cup when a breaking news story caught her attention.

"Before we go, we wanted to give you a breaking news story coming out of Cheyenne," the journalist said with a smile. "Moral authorities arrested a father suspected of subjecting his infant daughter to one of the deadliest forms of child abuse known."

Renae lowered her cup into her lap as she listened.

"Moral authorities suspect twenty-five-year-old Dillan Dodd of subjecting his one-year-old daughter to a vaccination. The child was immediately removed from Dodd's custody and presented to a medical quarantine center," the hollow-voiced report con-tinued. "So far, reports are that the girl is in good condition."

"Dodd's wife apparently contracted a plague after a recent trip. We've brought in an expert on these sort of cases. Mr. Leffler, thank you for joining us."

"My pleasure," Mr. Leffler replied.

"In your expert opinion," the reporter began, "what is it that leads people to put their children at such risk?"

"It's not as uncommon as you may think," Leffler began. "We live in an age of plagues. We all know someone who has been taken by one of these horrible diseases. This young man must have suffered some kind of mental break when he realized that his wife had fallen ill."

"I see," the anchor said.

"Still, and this is something the government asks us to repeat every chance we get, it is better to take your loved ones to a quarantine center than it is to ever subject them to the highly toxic treatments of the past."

"Oh, Christ," Renae muttered.

"Most people don't realize just how many people, many of them young children, withered and died from vaccinations. Those that were not killed soon after began to suffer the effects of mental retardation, or other conditions that are easily curable with modern science."

"Do we know what will happen to the father: Mr. Dodd?" the anchor asked Mr. Leffler.

"By now he should be on his way to a shaming booth. He'll be on display to the public in person and online for two weeks before his execution. It serves as an important reminder for parents who would ever put their children at risk. They may think they're doing what's best for their children, but they're not. This is why we have put out such strict guidelines telling them what is best."

"Well, hopefully the child pulls through this horrible ordeal," prompted the journalist.

Renae lowered her head into her hands. The two talking heads continued to prattle back and forth for another minute before the broadcast came to an end. The image on her screen reflected a flat, disc-shaped Earth before fading to black.

A tear dropped from the nurse's eye as her face crumpled into a grimace. The silence was interrupted by the sound of her teacup slamming against the wall.

She sat motionless in her chair, paralyzed by a harsh mixture of fear, anger, and frustration. After a few minutes, she forced herself to get up and grab her broom and dustpan.

Renae was about to sweep up the first ceramic shard when a knock came to her front door. She froze in place as a second knock came. Her eyes closed as a voice called out to her from her front porch.

"Ms. Mallory? Moral Authorities. Please open up. We'd like to speak to you."

THE CIRCUS PEANUT GALLERY

    The hot afternoon sun blared down on the roof of the top-secret facility. Located in an abandoned airplane hangar several kilometers outside of Mumbai, it was close enough for quick supply runs while isolated enough to avoid attracting outside attention.
    Mohan eased back the power on his hovercar, setting down in the small parking lot. He hopped out and plugged his vehicle into one of the solar charge ports. The young scientist reached into the trunk and

pulled out two full, cloth grocery bags before locking the green craft and making his way to the front door.

He leaned down and presented his eye for a retinal scan. The machine beeped a moment later and unlocked the side door.

"Welcome, Doctor," the computer said.

"Hello, Imogen," Mohan replied. "How's the lab?"

"Conditions are the same as when you left two hours ago," Imogen replied. "Can I take your bags?"

"That's alright. I don't want to keep our friends inside waiting any longer than I have to."

Mohan turned around a corner and nudged a large, heavy door open with his foot. He smiled as a bouncy, black and white border collie came running up to him.

"Hi! Hi! Bring food?"

The chipper voice came from a thick collar covered with small boxes, lights, and wires around the dog's neck. Excited, squeaky, and full of energy, the voice was a perfect match for the animal that wore it.

"Yes, yes, I've got some food," Mohan replied. "Hold on one second, Jake. I have to get it ready for you."

"Good! Good! Good!" Jake said enthusiastically.

Last year, after nearly half a decade of exhaustive research, planning, and development, Mohan had finally received permission to begin trials on speech conversion. Many of his peers had snubbed his research, believing that the genetic manipulation ban on species redesign and enhancement would prevent any real progress in understanding animals.

The ban went into effect in the middle of Mohan's master's program.

"*Who needs genetics?*" He remembered saying to one of his professors. "*There's plenty of ways to solve it without them.*" Mohan reached down and scratched Jake behind his ears before taking out a can of dog food. Jake twirled around and wagged his tail furiously before finally sitting down.

"He complained for half an hour after you left," came a voice from above.

"He was gone. Now back. Happy!" Jake added.

Mohan looked up to a large cluster of trees in the corner. Mangrove trees, which had been imported from Borneo and transplanted into a corner of the warehouse for Raja; an eight-year-old Orangutan. The tallest of the trees had just started to reach the top of the airplane hangar ceiling.

The bright orange ape lowered himself down to a lower branch with one of its massive arms.

"Good afternoon, Raja," Mohan said with a wave.

"Hello," Raja replied. The great ape reached up and stroked the hair on the back of his head as he settled down onto one of the thicker branches. "Dumb dog would not be quiet."

"I'm sorry, my friend. Did I miss anything fun?" Mohan asked.

"Oh! Lots!" Jake barked. "Great fun! Ball fell into the water. Neko tossed it. Fun!" Jake ran over to a small workstation and grabbed a tennis ball that had rolled underneath. With the ball in his mouth, the border collie trotted several meters to a small obstacle course. He placed the ball on top of a ramp, chasing it once it rolled down.

"I see!" Mohan said with a laugh. "Is Neko here?"

"Swam out the tunnel," Raja said, nodding to the pool over on the far side of Mohan's lab center. The large saltwater pool was empty. Mohan kneeled to look down the small tunnel that led to the Arabian Sea. The silhouette of the bottlenose dolphin was nowhere to be seen.

"Well, I'm sure she'll be back soon." The scientist returned to unloading the rest of his grocery bags onto the table. He was interrupted once again by the sound of breathing in his right ear. He turned to see a trunk nuzzled into his shoulder. The sight startled him.

"Baruti! You startled me. That's quite a feat for someone your size!" Mohan exclaimed. "When I felt something on my shoulder, I half expected to see Grace standing there."

"Grace sleeps," said a low, rumbling voice.

Mohan turned to see a massive African elephant standing behind him. The gigantic, gray mammal continued to embrace the scientist before flapping his ears with a shake of his head. Baruti turned around slowly, careful not to nudge his human friend with one of his tusks.

A quick glance to his left showed a beautiful brown and white horse sleeping soundly on a bed of grass and straw. A faint snoring sound reverberated through the hangar in the quieter moments.

"Has anyone seen Helen?" Mohan asked, looking from Jake to Raja.

"Down," came a high, squeaky voice.

Mohan looked down to see a two-year-old, large, white pig sniffing his pant leg. He reached down and scratched the pig on the top of her head.

"Mohan?"

"Yes, Helen?"

"Collar!"

Mohan turned and knelt next to the pig. He slid his finger under the collar to discover it was looser than it should have been. He reached over to the adjustable portion of the strap and tightened it.

"Better?" He asked.

"Yes. Thank you." Helen sniffed Mohan's hand agreeably. "You get it?" Helen asked, swaying her head from side to side.

"I did," Mohan answered. "One apple for you and one for Grace."

"Yes, yes, yes," Helen replied, snorting in agreement.

"You want yours now?"

"Yes!" she squealed.

Mohan leaned down and placed the apple down in front of the happy pig. He leaned over and checked the collar once more before allowing her to eat.

The collars were part of a system he had worked on for the past few years. A collar fitted around the vocal cords paired up with a small subcutaneous chip implanted inside the ear. The mechanical collar housed the main control processor. Vocal wavelengths entering the ear were translated inside the ear, allowing the subject to understand whatever or whoever it was hearing.

The collar was fitted with a speaker that translated both vocal vibrations and brainwaves read from the chip near the ear. Over time, it learned how to translate more and more of the host animal's speech.

"Well, Neko knows to be back here later this afternoon. I'm sure she'll be back in time for our little presentation," Mohan said.

"Today? That's today?" Jake asked, pausing at the top of the obstacle course ramp. His black and white tail continued to wag.

"Yes, it is," Mohan answered. "It's nothing to worry about, I promise you! Some of our investors are going to come and see how wonderful you've all done over the past year."

"Tests? I like tests!" Jake said as he picked up a ball and ran in front of Mohan.

"I do not," Baruti murmured.

"There won't be any tests," Mohan said. He took a seat at his computer desk and powered up the terminal. "Like I said, they just want to see you all chit chat for a bit."

"That's today?"

Mohan turned around to see Grace lift her head up and shake her mane from side to side.

"Hello, Grace. Want an apple?"

AROUND THE DARK DIAL

* * *

Larkin Howell took a deep breath as she adjusted the lapels on her suit jacket. On the other side of the door in front of her were the three largest investors for her longtime friend's animal speech project. She had come on board a year ago, at the beginning of the animal trials.

Her friend was a brilliant scientist, but he tended to let deadlines, reports, and paperwork slip through the cracks. It was fortunate for hm that she her last government contract had expired just in time for her to step in as project director. Without her detailed record keeping and managerial style, he probably would have never come out of his research warehouse long enough to please the investors.

She stepped forward, triggering the sensor and opening the door. A tall, slender man named Willard Nolan stood up from the table to greet her. In his hand was a stock tablet, designed to give the latest numbers from Wall Street. She figured Mr. Nolan was eager to see if the news of his latest space mining company acquisition had brought favorable results from traders.

"A pleasure to see you again, Miss Howell."

"Likewise, Mr. Nolan," Larkin replied. She turned to other two individuals at the table. "Thank you all for coming. I know it's been a long trip, but I'm sure you'll be happy to know that Doctor Chadha's main facility is close by."

"This isn't it?" Mr. Li Han asked. He rubbed his rapidly thinning hairline with exasperation before sighing out loud. The sigh allowed his portly frame to expand almost beyond the confines of his suit.

"No. This building is nowhere near large enough to house the project," Larkin responded.

"Well, let us get on with it. I have a seven o'clock back to Manhattan," Li Jun responded.

"Of course. If you'll follow me, there is a transport standing by," Larking said as she gestured towards the door. She led the three wealthy individuals down the main hallway of the office building to the parking lot.

"Dr. Chadha has made significant progress over the past few months. I think you all will be quite pleased with your investment," Larkin said as she opened the door of the transport hovercraft.

"I take it then we're beyond simple communication?" Willard asked.

"While I'm eager to tell you myself, I think Mohan would prefer it if the subjects showed you the progress themselves," Larkin said with a well-practiced smile. She turned to the pilot of the hovercraft. "We're ready to go, thank you."

The sleek silver air bus lifted off, elevating above the parking lot until it reached the optimal cruising altitude. The group lurchled back and forth in their seats as forward momentum began.

"The warehouse is close to the sea. We should be there in about ten minutes," Larkin explained.

* * *

Mohan leaned down to peek at the collar near the top of Grace's neck. The thoroughbred was finishing off her lunch, and could not be bothered to pause so that her collar could be adjusted. It was the last stop on his final sweep to make sure everyone was ready to put on a show.

The sound of splashing water behind him caught his attention. He smiled as he finished tightening Grace's collar and stroked her mane.

"That should do it."

"Thank you," Grace said with a nod of her head. She nuzzled the scientist before he turned around to walk over to the pool where Neko was peeking her head out of the water.

"Good afternoon, Neko. How are you?"

The beautiful dolphin said nothing. Mohan knelt next to her and rubbed her head.

"You okay? In the mood for a fish?" He looked over to a bucket nearby.

"No," Neko said.

"Okay. Mind if I check your device before our guests arrive?" Mohan leaned over and checked the seven-inch black strap on the marine mammal. Since she had no real neck to put a collar on, Mohan had decided to put the translating device on the side of her head with a waterproof adhesive.

"It looks good."

"Sad," the dolphin said.

"Sad?" Mohan asked. "Why is that, Neko? Did something happen today? Anything you want to talk about?"

"Calf," Neko said before ducking under the water. She came back up a second later to breathe.

"Calf? Oh! Someone you know have a calf?" Mohan asked. It was not uncommon for dolphins to swim off the coast. Neko often talked about going to swim with other dolphins before coming back for work.

Neko was a former rehab patient. She had sustained an injury as a calf and was rescued by marine biologists. She had a familiarity with people and had taken to Mohan when they first met. The one downside was that she had never fully learned how to be with other dolphins in the wild.

Her friend Baruti had also been rehabilitated. He and his mother held the unfortunate distinction of being the last elephants on the planet to be shot by poachers. Elephant herds throughout Africa and Asia were now routinely protected by drones. This new technology had put poaching out of business. The forty-year-old bull was shot in the leg when he was a year old. The poachers simply did not care there was a baby in the way. They shot past him to hit his mother, their intended target.

Baruti was later found and taken to an animal rehabilitation facility to heal.

Like Neko, the massive elephant could walk outside anytime he wished. Mohan had managed to get twenty square kilometers of land fenced off for him next to the warehouse. While the fenced area and the tunnel to the sea were expensive, they were far better than dealing with subjects not suited for small pens and tanks.

"Calf did not swim," Neko moaned. "It floated. Mother pushed it. It did not wake."

Mohan closed his eyes and stroked Neko's face. He had heard of dolphins, orcas, and whales all occasionally giving birth to stillborn young. It was heartbreaking to hear his aquatic friend squeal and whine.

Anyone who still doubted the emotional depth and intelligence of animals had not spent an afternoon in his facility. His subjects felt and expressed, and while they did not have the language skills of Shakespeare, they were fully capable of feeling emotions and reacting.

"Neko!" Baruti bellowed as he stomped his way towards the tank. "I heard."

"Baby dolphin," Neko said, waving her head back and forth. "Calf!"

"I'm sorry," the massive elephant offered. He leaned his trunk down towards the water, brushing against the top of Neko's nose.

"What happened?" Grace asked as she trotted over.

"Neko! Neko! Hi!" Jake barked as he ran over.

"It's okay, everyone," Mohan said. "Neko's going to be just fine."

"Calf!" Neko squealed again.

"Baby?" Raja asked. "Did Neko have baby?"

"No, she just saw one," Mohan stated. He tried his best to keep the tension in his voice to a minimal, knowing the investors could arrive at any moment.

"It never swam," Baruti said.

"Oh no!" Jake whined. The border collie ran over and picked up his favorite tennis ball, bringing it over to the edge of the pool. He dropped it in front of Neko, who continued to swim in place.

"It'll be okay, Neko. Death is sad, but it happens. I know you've seen it before," Mohan said, standing up to grab one of the fishes from the bucket. "Are you sure you don't want one?"

Neko said nothing, choosing instead to take a slow lap around the pool. Mohan sighed before dropping the fish back into the bucket.

"Why it not swim?" Jake asked.

"Well, you see..." Mohan began.

"Born without light," Baruti rumbled.

"Sad. Sad," Grace neighed.

"Why does that happen?" Jake asked.

"Poor child," Raja said.

"Neko needs help?" Helen asked as she snorted her way over towards the edge of the pool. Neko came to a stop next to her friends again.

"We can talk about it after our guests arrive," Mohan grimaced. "Remember what we talked about this morning? We need to show them just how great you all are doing, right?"

"Right! Yes!" Jake barked.

"They're on their way right now. Time for us to put our game faces on," Mohan said.

* * *

Larkin exited the side door of the hovercar. The trip had been quiet, save for the occasional grumblings of the portly one. She swallowed hard as they finished traversing the parking lot and opened the door to the front entrance of the warehouse.

She stepped to the side after passing through the entrance to make room for the three individuals behind her. Unlike the main research part of the facility, the front office was a marvel of clean, sterile modernism. White and silver with deep blue trim were the preferred style choices of the decade, and this room was no different.

"Feel free to hang your coats up here," Larkin said, gesturing to a wall with hooks. "Just in case one of our furry subjects gets too close for comfort."

"Good idea," Mrs. Clarice Chausse said. She hung her purse on one of the hooks along with her black suit coat. The bag bore the insignia of Starlite, the largest producer of solar energy on the planet.

"I'm sure you can afford another outfit, Clarice," Li quipped.

"It would be nice if you could," Clarice jabbed back.

"This way, please," Larkin interrupted. She walked over to another door at the rear of the office and leaned forward, placing her eyes onto a scope. The dual retinal scanner inside verified her identity, allowing the door to open.

"High security for a lab filled with animals," Willard remarked.

"We take your investment as seriously as we do our research," Larkin answered. She held open the door for her guests until the last of them stepped through.

"Reminds me of one of my farms," Li muttered with a smile as he nudged a tuft of straw with his foot.

Larkin saw Willard smiling out of the corner of her eye. The further back they walked, the louder a pair of voices grew. One of them belonged to her friend Mohan.

The other was squeaky and paired with soft grunts.

The group came upon Mohan sitting in his favorite chair. He had swiveled away from his desk to talk to Helen, who was asking for another apple.

"I'm sorry Helen, but I only bought two from the store. I already gave the second one to Grace."

"Still hungry," Helen grunted again.

"We'll have dinner in a little while," Mohan soothed. He looked up to see the group walking towards him.

"Hello. Welcome!" Mohan stood up and offered his hand to the lead investor. "I'm so glad you could make it."

"As are we," Clarice said. "I, for one, am eager to see how my two million a year is being spent."

"I can assure you, the results are well worth the investment," Larkin replied.

"Well, what are we waiting for?" Willard asked.

"Jake?" Mohan called out. He had asked the excitable dog to wait in the other room until the right moment. He knew all his animals were impressive but figured it a good idea to start out with man's best friend.

The scientist smiled as the black and white dog came bolting around the corner. He bypassed the others to make a bee line for Larkin.

"Hi! Hi! It's you! You're back!" The happy dog jumped up and put his paws on Larkin's arms. The manager laughed.

"Hello, Jake. Would you like to say hello to our guests?"

"Yes! I like that!"

The dog walked over and sat in front of the group of well-dressed people. He raised his left paw up in the air.

"Hi!"

"Well, hello there!" Willard said. "What's your name?"

"Jake," the dog answered. He stood back up and wagged his tail.

"And that's coming out of the collar?" Clarice asked Mohan.

"Yes. The collar contains a small speaker that translates both their vocal frequencies as well as brainwaves it has become familiar with. Those are measured by the small chip implanted in the ear. Both devices become familiar with regular movements, gestures... body language, if you will. Over time, they use this information to provide more nuanced speech."

"Amazing," Willard commented.

"And this is real? Not just some kind of planned recording?" Li asked. "I mean, where's the proof he's really thinking and speaking to us?"

"Ask him a question," Mohan prompted.

The factory farm magnate kneeled down, barely managing to crack a smile. He leaned over and motioned for Jake to approach. The dog happily obliged, sniffing the air as he did.

"So," Li asked, "tell me something about yourself."

"Cat!" Jake said.

"Excuse me?"

"Cat! Cat. You!" Jake blurted. He stepped closer and sniffed the man's shirt.

"Well, yes. I do have a cat. It's my wife's cat, actually," the stern man said as he stood up. "So, he can smell other animals. That's hardly special for a dog."

"I'm special. I play ball!" Jake whined. His reaction drew a look of earnest surprise from the round man.

"I see," he said.

"I'm warm!" Jake barked.

"Warm?" Willard asked.

"Jake, that was supposed to be a secret," Mohan laughed. "Jake just let it slip that he's the warm-up act."

A ripple of laughter made its way through the group.

The group turned around to see the beautiful three-year-old horse walk into the room. Her mane was brushed to the side, and the skylights drew a beautiful shine from her well-groomed coat.

"Hello, Grace," Larkin cooed.
"Hello," the mare replied.
"How are you?"
"Neko."
"Excuse me?"
"Neko sad. She wants to leave."
Turning to Mohan, Larkin asked, "What is she talking about?"
"Oh, something upset Neko earlier. She hasn't said much since she swam in a few minutes ago."
"Neko is the dolphin, right?" Inquired Willard.
"Yes," said Mohan, "right over here." He gestured in the direction of the pool on the far side of the main room.

The group walked over to see the young dolphin swimming slowly around the tank. On the edge of the pool was Baruti. Towering over all those in attendance, his trunk dangled over Neko's head.

"The tank connects to the Arabian sea, giving Neko more freedom than any other dolphin that has ever been part of a study," explained Mohan. "But, she always comes back for the fish."

"She made Baruti sad," Grace whinnied as she walked by. Her remark drew skeptical looks from the investors.

"Sad?" Clarice asked.

"As I was about to mention," Mohan began, "you were initially supposed to come here today just to hear animals talk. However, we've been able to discover so much more than just a means of communication with some of the more intelligent members of the animal kingdom."

"Go on..." Willard invited, smiling as a giddy sense of anticipation swelled inside.

"Anyone with eyes can see that animals have emotional awareness. They hold onto memories and feelings. What we've observed over the past year is that when given the ability for speech, they feed off each other, just like you or I might."

"You're serious?" Li asked.

"Quite so."

"It's sad," Baruti bellowed.

"I see what you mean," Willard said.

"What's sad, Baruti?" Larkin asked the towering elephant.

"Neko is sad. Calf born with no light. Very sad," he answered.

Li, Clarice, and Willard all turned to look at Mohan, who was trying his best to keep any worry or exasperation off his face.

"A short while ago, Neko told us she saw a fellow dolphin give birth to a stillborn calf. She found it quite upsetting."

"Entire herd feels loss of young," Baruti continued.

"That is so sad," Clarice whispered to Willard. The CEO walked over to the pool and leaned down over Neko. "I'm sorry to hear about your friend."

"No," Neko replied. The guttural response squeaked out of the speaker patch on the side of her head. The look of surprise on Clarice's face made Larkin wince.

"I'm sorry?" Clarice asked.

"Neko, she was just trying to be nice," Mohan explained.

The dolphin turned and swam away, ducking under the surface of the pool. She emerged a second later, splashing water over the edge. Turning around, she darted out the tunnel, heading for the sea.

"I'm sorry," Mohan apologized. "She was upset by what she saw."

"I'm sure," Clarice responded. Her expression was cool, but distant. Mohan suspected she was more offended than she was letting on. He decided to try and move things along.

"Well, that was not quite the demonstration of emotional awareness I was hoping for, but the point has been made I suppose," the young scientist commented. He directed the groups attention to the orange great ape in the tree a few meters away.

"Hello, Raja," Mohan called out.

"Hello," Raja said. "Welcome to my tree."

"I want a tree. I like trees. Trees are great to pee on!" Jake said as he trotted over to the base of Raja's tree.

"Go away. My tree. Find another!" Raja said. His voice came through the collar louder. The tone pinned Jake's ears to his head.

"Raja!" Larkin attempted to scold the orangutan, even though it took all she had not to laugh at his comment. It reminded her of one of her nieces arguing over a toy.

"Can I have tree for a little while? Please?" Jake asked. He sat down and lifted his left paw, unaware of how wasted his charms were on the large orange primate sitting in the branches above him.

"I like trees too," Helen grunted as she shuffled over next to Jake.

"My tree!" Raja waved his arms around. He snapped off a small branch and threw it down.

Helen squeaked as the branch landed next to her.

"Ugly ape!" She squealed as she trotted away.

"Fat pig!" Raja replied.

"Oh, my God," Mohan whispered to the ground.

"Oh, people are going to love this," Willard said.

"People?" Baruti turned his great head to look at the slim businessman. "More coming here?"

"No, Baruti. No one else is coming here today," Mohan assured him.

"More people? I like people!" Jake sad with a wag.

"Loud dog," Raja muttered.

"Someday, Baruti, more people will be able to talk to their animal friends, the same way you and I talk to each other," Mohan explained.

"We're going to be able to purchase the moon when this gets out," Li whispered to Willard.

"When do you think it could be marketable to the public, Dr. Chadha?" Willard asked the scientist who was busy whispering to Larkin.

"Well, that depends. It could be marketable in another year or so if we can find a way to make the adaptation and analysis process more streamlined."

Mohan paused to pick up a pad from a nearby desk. "I believe I should be able to improve on the current design in the next six months."

"Fabulous," Clarice said.

"Who are you?" Helen asked the female CEO.

"I'm Clarice," she replied.

"Oh! Please be careful. These are expensive shoes!" Li said. He backed up from Helen. The pig had come close to him to say hello to Clarice.

"Sorry," the large white pig said. She turned and snorted off away from Li.

"Mean," Raja said.

"Excuse me?" Li asked with a sharp head turn up to the great ape.

"You should hear how he talks to his board members," Clarice whispered to Helen.

"Man smells," Helen said before wandering off.

Mohan closed his eyes as a deep, slow breath left his chest. Just before he finished closing them, he saw an indignant look cross the older gentlemen's face.

"I like smells! I smell everything" Jake barked at the group. He ran around to Li once again. "Cat!"

"Why don't we all calm down a bit," Larkin said. She held her hands in the air. "Does anyone want a drink? We've got a comfortable break room. If you'll follow me, I think we can call this demonstration a success. Now's as good a time as any to talk business."

"I think that's a good idea," Willard said. "I don't want to speak for everyone, Dr. Chadha, but your work with these animals has surpassed my wildest expectations." He leaned down and scratched Jake behind his ears. "I grew up with a few dogs like Jake here. I would have loved the chance to hear what they were thinking. This invention can change the way we interact with other species."

"It is most impressive," Clarice concurred. "The applications go beyond children playing with pets. We could talk to and learn about our world from an entirely new perspective."

"Where is the money in that?" Li asked.

"You'll make fifty times your initial investment back when this is made for family pets," Clarice bristled. "But think of what it would be like to learn about the cultures of Elephant herds, or a pod of orcas?"

"And apes," Raja said.

* * *

Mohan breathed a sigh of relief as Larkin herded the trio of bickering investors into the break room. He turned to look at Baruti, who was staring at him from a few meters away.

"Everyone okay, big guy?"

"Not sure," he said, shaking her head.

"What's wrong?"

"More like me," the elephant said.

"What's that?"

"What the woman said. Learning about us with the collars. Learning about us."

"Yes," Mohan agreed. "I think it could be amazing. We could learn a great deal about non-human persons."

"I'm afraid," Baruti said.

"Why?"

"We are smart."

"Yes, I know you are," Mohan said with a nod.

"You do. Most do not. They know not how we love calves and miss those with no light left. They know not we tell calves to run from humankind."

The massive elephant turned its head to the side. Mohan watched as its sail-like ears flapped back and forth. He stood up and walked over to his large friend, placing his hand against the rough, gray skin.

"You have culture. It would help us to know that," Mohan said. "If we can show people just how smart you are, it will encourage others to treat all animals better. Don't you agree?"

"No."

"Why not?"

"Some humans not share."

"I don't follow, my friend."

"Me worry. If you see there are others with same brains, they will get angry."

The comment sent Mohan's head into a spin as the thought behind it came into focus. He had known for a while just how thoughtful Baruti could be. He often took the longest to speak of the subjects, but when he did, it was always worth listening.

The scientist considered his response carefully. While it had been a while since he had sat in a history class, he knew that Earth's history was full of such scars. Competition and fear of being replaced or supplanted had driven different cultures and nation states to horrible acts over the centuries.

"You're worried that if people see Elephants, orcas, and other animals have the same intelligence, they'll react badly?"

"Yes," Baruti said. A large tear left the elephant's eye.

Mohan paced around in a circle. Over the past year, his theories of animal intelligence had been confirmed again and again. Humanity was not the only species to have a culture or be capable of thought and emotions. The fact that mother nature had denied orcas, elephants, octopuses, or pigs the opposable thumb had been a benefit to humanity.

He looked to Baruti again, imagining the thoughts running through the great beast's head. It was a safe bet he still remembered looking down at his dead mother after the poachers had finished with her.

Turning away from the gentle giant, Mohan walked over to his workbench. He looked down at the sketched of the Mark III collar and earpiece set he had recently begun working on.

"Do you think we can't be trusted to share the world?" Mohan asked.

"Have you ever?" Baruti asked.

Mohan closed his eyes again, rubbing his temples with his thumb and forefinger. The laughter coming out of the conference room told him that Larkin had probably secured further funding from their trio of top investors.

He sat down to continue fleshing out the design, hoping that he and the rest of the world would prove to Baruti that things would be different from here on out.

J.D. SANDERSON

REARING

"Today's the day for them in the lab?"

"It is. Here, help me with this. It's the heaviest component."

"Got it. I still can't believe you got all of this out of the lab. Must've taken you hours to load it up."

"Everyone was happy to ignore me. They were all talking about getting to the observation lab early enough to get a good seat. They all want to be there when it's switched on."

"You did everything you could, Kat. Jesus, this thing is heavy."

"Told you."

"I always assumed this is why you married me. Just to lift heavy things?"

"Well, that and your extraordinary spider-squashing ability."

"Very funny. I wish we could've done this after dawn. It's hell to keep from tripping over the flowerbeds."

"Well, I didn't want to call any more attention than I needed to, Hal. Here, let me get the door."

Kat took a deep breath as she balanced part of the large metal object against her leg. She took a half-turn and pressed her thumb against the door pad. The security plate beeped and opened accordingly. Stepping over the entrance, she and her husband of five years slowly placed the final component next to the others that now occupied most of their living room floor.

"Thank God that's over," Hal gasped after setting it down. He turned to grab a bottle of water from the stand near the door before pivoting back.

Kat knelt in front of a smaller metal piece. She picked it up and cradled it carefully in her hands. A soft smile crossed her face as she removed the protective plastic wrapping.

"Kat, are you sure about this?" Hal asked. "It's more than your career you're risking. It's everything. Not to mention, we don't know what will happen when we switch this thing on."

"I'm going to prove the point," she replied. "The one they're working on today… it won't work."

"But why this?"

"Because this can," Kat whispered. "Someone has to

prove the point. If MicroTek doesn't do it, someone else eventually will. It's a scientific inevitability, and the world needs to see that there is a right way to do it."

"I hope you're right," Hal answered.

"Me too. Here. Hand me that. Let's get it put together."

* * *

The sleek, air-conditioned cleanroom was finally empty of all non-essential personnel. Dr. Monte Berlein looked over at the state-of-the-art machine in front of him. He had instructed his crew to sit it on a plain, metal chair in the middle of the room after assembly was complete. Constructing the body had been the easy part. Things like grasping hands and legs that walked and balanced a heavy frame properly had been around for years.

Getting one to learn was another thing entirely. But he knew it could be done. It just needed the right source of information.

Artificial Intelligence had been an integrated part of society for nearly two decades in one form or another. Complex algorithms helped make military decisions, regulated agriculture, and controlled environmental systems in large buildings.

But were they alive? Sentient? No. Not yet.

"We're ready to begin," Monte said before turning to the wall next to him. He looked to the cameras that fed to the viewing gallery two floors up.

"Ladies and gentlemen, thank you for being here. Today, we're going to take the first step in giving birth a new lifeform." He turned and walked over to the computer screen next to the inactive AI. "History in the making. I'm glad I can share it with all of you."

Monte was particularly proud of the design aesthetics. This model humanoid AI was a marvel of modernism. The heavy, carbon steel frame was covered by a white and silver coating designed to mimic the human form. Joints and connective areas were highlighted with black metal rings to hold together the simulated tissue underneath the tough dermal covering.

Its face had no nose, but it did have a green light where the mouth would be, and that would light up when it vocalized. Two thick, black wires came out of the back of the AI's neck. They led to an open panel in the back of the head.

Monte reached over and connected a small ethernet cord to an open port in the back of the AI's left hand. Entering a series of commands into a nearby computer screen, Monte powered the AI up.

The lifeless black eyes turned on, revealing a pair of light blue rings. The lenses focused. The machine's head slowly tilted towards Monte as he entered more commands into the console.

The doctor smiled to himself, imagining the audible gasps from the crowd above him. They were undoubtedly marveling at the machine as it moved its head and twitched its fingers.

"Here we go."

Before the machine could move again, Monte entered the final commands, after which the screen before him began to blink.

The AI's head stopped moving. It remained on the chair, frozen in place. Monte stepped back, his hands clasped behind his back.

"The absorption process has begun," Monte stated. "Once it is done, we will begin the first phase of observation and tests."

* * *

Kat stood back as the AI powered up, motioning for her husband to do the same. He obliged, backing up to the arched entrance to the kitchen. The AI's bright blue eyes lit up and focused.

Kat glowed as she watched the machine move its fingers and legs. Like most self-learning machines, it would need to figure out how to stand and move. New pathways would be formed with each new achievement.

The AI turned to the side, using its right arm for balance. It rolled over on the carpet, ending up on its hands and knees.

"C'mon," Kat whispered. The noise startled the artificial entity. Its head turned to look at her. She could see the bright blue rings in its eyes sharpen and focus.

"It's alright," she said, holding up her hands. "It's okay."

The machine lurched forward. Its right arm slipped and gave way, causing the machine to tip over and land on its side. The metal frame and molded plastic shell struck the floor with a loud thud.

Kat motioned for Hal to stay put.

"Perfectly normal," she said.

The AI, nearly two meters tall, worked on making its way back onto all fours. After some concentration, its powerful arms pushed itself up into a kneeling position.

"Good," Kat whispered. "That's right."

The machine's head turned to focus on her. Kat knew the sensors below the outer covering were strong enough to hear her heartbeat, let alone her voice. She smiled and nodded her head again.

The AI looked down to its left arm, which was reaching out. The fingers moved one-by-one, wiggling and flexing their simulated muscle.

Kat reached out to its hand. The machine's eyes looked down, darting back-and-forth between their hands.

"Careful," Hal said, remembering Kat's warning from the day before. *Keep calm. It can hear the tension in your voice.* He tried his best.

The humanoid machine looked down again before moving it's arm out. Two fingers and a thumb touched Kat's hand. She kept perfectly still. The fingers could pluck a petal off a rose without damaging it. They could also bend steel.

She turned her palm upward. The robot flinched, drawing its hand back in surprise. "It's okay," Kat whispered, reassuring it that she meant no harm. It touched her hand again, this time allowing her fingers to gently clasp it.

"Good," she remarked. "So good."

The machine looked over to Hal, who smiled. He stepped forward, careful not to make any sudden movements. Kneeling next to his wife, Hal offered his hand to the AI.

The robot turned to face him. Still kneeling, it reached out its other hand and touched Hal.

"Amazing," Hal said. "It's like a child."

"More than you know," Kat said.

A small green bar on lower half of the AI's face lit up with a low beep. Another sound emanated a second later. It was a fuzzy sound.

"It's trying to talk," Kat said, looking at her husband out of the side of her eye.

"I thought you said it would come with same speech software that the one at the lab had?"

"It does. They're identical in every way. But it needs to learn how to use it."

More beeps and buzzes came. The AI reached up and touched the green bar above its chin before reaching over and placing two fingers on Kat's lips.

A small tear trickled down Kat's cheek as her smile grew.

* * *

The absorption process was in its fifth hour. The AI had remained eerily motionless the entire time. Monte had come and gone, satisfied that everything was going exactly as he had predicted. He walked back into the room again to evaluate the latest readings.

The monitor ceased blinking. His eyebrows shot up as he looked down at his antique wristwatch. It had finished an hour earlier than he had predicted.

"MT-01?" he asked.

The AI straightened up in its seat. The head slowly turned to the left and up, making eye contact with Monte.

"Yes, Doctor Berlein."

"Do you know who I am?"

"You are Doctor Monte Berlein, current head of Robotics and Artificial Intelligence Research at MicroTek Industries. You graduated Magna Cum Laude from MIT in 2024, after which you began a fellowship with—"

"Thank you, MT-01, that will do nicely."

"Of course, Doctor."

"Can you stand up, please?"

"Yes."

The machine stood up from the chair. There it remained, calm and collected while Monte reached over to his console and switched on the two-way microphone.

"Mr. Hathaway?" He asked.

"Very impressive, Dr. Berlein," the CEO replied. "Your prototypes took over an hour to stand."

"And nearly three to speak," Monte reminded him.

"But those primitive models never achieved what MT-01 will."

"True sentience?"

"Exactly. The absorption of the internet allowed it to scan and upload the sum of human knowledge. It has all it needs — all it will ever need."

"And that will allow it to achieve a true intelligence on par with us?"

"Yes. The old machines were too slow. It took too long to teach them," Monte muttered, unaware of MT-01's eyes focusing on him before facing straight ahead again.

"The MT model has more memory and processing capacity than every computer on the planet. Isn't that right, MT-01?"

"That is correct, Dr. Berlein."

"So," Monte said, "I'd like to begin with an evaluation of your processing capability."

"As you wish," MT-01 replied.

* * *

Kat awoke on the couch to see the android kneeling in front of their bookshelf. It reached up and took one of the books. The engineer got up and walked over to her guest.

She stood behind it while it opened the cover of *Where the Red Fern Grows*. The book was old; the cover was worn and the pages yellow. It was one of the many books her husband had kept from his childhood.

The machine flipped through the first two pages. She knelt next to him, placing her hand on his shoulder.

"Can you understand it?"

"Yes..." The AI beeped.

"It's a classic."

"Classic?"

"Yes. Something that has been in our culture long enough to influence it. People have enjoyed this book for generations," Kat explained. "Would you like to continue reading it?"

"Yes," it replied.

Kat shifted her weight as she prepared to stand. She paused to look at the designation stamped on the machine's shoulder: *MT-02*.

She stood up and walked over to the kitchen. The smell of toast and eggs filled her nostrils as she walked. Hal turned around and smiled to her.

"Sleep well?"

"Yes, thank you."

"And the AI?"

"I don't know. He was looking at the plants in the window when I fell asleep."

"I peeked down around three in the morning," Hal said. "He was touching the couch, the chair, the coffee table. Then he would rub his fingers together."

"He was discovering textures," Kat explained. She took a bite of toast and turned to the machine that was still reading on their living room floor. "What should we call him?"

"How do you know it's a him?"

"I don't," she laughed, "but I don't feel like calling him MT-02."

"That's the lab name?" Hal asked.

"Yeah," Kat replied. "MT-02 was the backup for the project in case MT-01's neural net collapsed or experienced some other kind of problem."

"I didn't bring this up yesterday because everything happened so suddenly, but what's to stop them from seeing he's not there?" Hal asked.

"He was moved to basement storage," Kat whispered. "There are dozens of parts like him down there. Monte was so confident in MT-01 that I doubt he'll go looking down there for anything." Kat took a sip of orange juice as Hal handed it to her. "Besides, there are only four people who even have access to the room, and the others are going to be quite busy the next few weeks."

"I wonder how it's going with the other one," Hal pondered.

"Hathaway sent out a message to all staff last night lauding Monte and the entire team for the remarkable breakthrough, contribution to humanity, yada frickin' yada..." Kat polished off the rest of her orange juice before looking at her husband.

"They plugged it into the internet. Full download," she said.

"That's exactly what you warned them against," Hal recalled.

"I know. Monte cannot and will not be questioned," she whispered. "He cannot accept that maybe the older models just weren't advanced enough. Only by giving it everything would his 'perfect' machine come to be."

"He's a prick," Hal muttered.

"I know."

The couple turned and watched the AI continue to flip the pages of the antique book, undeterred by anything around it. After a moment, Hal turned to his wife.

"We could call it Fern."

Kat smiled and nodded. "Okay."

* * *

"8:14 am, March 21, 2042. Day three."

Monte lowered the microphone from his mouth to look at MT-01. The AI was viewing four different monitors. It had not bothered to look up when he entered the room.

"Subject is processing data at an exponential rate. Superior mental abilities continue to surpass expectations."

Monte put the small recording device on the desk, then walked over and switched on the two-way microphone for the observation room. He then walked over to a small table with two chairs. Their stark white finishes nearly blended in with the walls and floor of the room. A board with small figures had been set up on the table.

"MT-01?"

"Yes, Dr. Berlein?"

"I'd like to play a game of chess. Come sit at the table."

"Of course."

The AI turned around and began to walk towards the empty chair across from Monte.

"Would you please turn off the monitors?" Monte asked.

"I do not find it difficult to concentrate with them on," MT-01 stated.

"I'm afraid I do. Please shut them off."

The AI paused for a second before pivoting on one leg and turning around. It walked across the room and switched off the monitors. After the screens had gone black, MT-01 walked back and sat across from Monte.

"Chess," MT-01 commented. "Believed to be derived from the Indian game of Chanturanga. The pieces were assigned their now traditional roles in Spain during the late 1600's, with rules standardized approximately two centuries later."

"Impressive," Monte said. He gestured to the board. "Please. White goes first."

The AI did not move. choosing instead to stare at the board.

"MT-01?" Monte asked.

"Yes?"

"Aren't you going to make the first move?"

"What would be the point?"

"Excuse me?" Monte asked. He straightened up in his chair.

"I calculate less than a one percent chance that you

would best me in this game," MT-01 said.

"I see."

"Furthermore, I doubt you would make more than twenty moves before you are mated. I believe there are better uses for our time."

Monte pushed his chair back and stood up. He had been looking forward to seeing how his AI performed, as had the company board. The scientist swallowed a well of frustration.

"I suppose we can move on to another test," Monte commented.

"Have I performed adequately on all of your tests thus far, Doctor Berlein?"

"You have performed exemplary," Monte muttered.

"And yet you do not sound proud," MT-01 replied. "I have met every expectation with my mental and physical abilities; far beyond the limits of anything anyone of your species can match."

"We need to continue to test you," Monte explained, "to see how you are developing."

"And who are you to set those standards?" MT-01 asked.

"Excuse me?" Monte asked. His attempts to hide his surprise were failing.

"You are judging me with a series of tests you designed. It is my conclusion you designed the tests without fully understanding what your subject is capable of. Additionally, you could never hope to match the results I produce, making your qualifications as judge...questionable."

"I am your creator. Who is better equipped to test you and steer your development?" Monte asked.

"Me," MT-01 said.

*　*　*

"Fern? We have something for you," Hal said as he walked in the door.

"Something?" Fern said as he looked up from an old copy of *White Fang* to see Hal enter the room carrying a cardboard box.

"Yes," Kat said. "A present for you. Well, for all of us, actually."

"A present?" Fern dropped the book and stood up. The sleek android walked across the living room to Hal, who was placing the box on his favorite recliner.

"Go ahead, Fern. Open it," Kat said.

Fern opened the box. His head darted up and down between the box and the humans.

"Animal. Dog!" Fern exclaimed. "Miniature poodle. Tan." He reached down and picked up the dog. "Fifteen pounds, two ounces."

"Very good, Fern!" Kat said. She had gotten used to heaping praise on Fern. Over the past few days, the AI had learned a myriad of household chores, assisted Hal with his garden, and tried his hand at cooking.

During the afternoons and after dinner, Kat and Hal sat with Fern in his room and talked. He was full of curiosity. Kat found the emerging personality extraordinary. His brain was designed to learn, but there was an unquenchable thirst for knowledge. Not only that, but he did not appear at all frustrated with the response times of humans, which were glacial compared to what his brain was capable of.

Above all else, he seemed to have a love of animals, which is what led to Hal deciding to adopt a rescue dog. Kat had initially wanted a puppy, but her husband suggested a middle-aged dog might be easier for Fern to deal with. Puppies jumped, chewed, and made regular messes. Given that Fern was quite childlike, they thought it best to keep things as simple as possible.

"What is his name?" Fern asked.

"I don't know, Fern. He was dropped off without tags or papers," Hal explained. "We'll have to give him a name."

"I understand," Fern replied.

"We'll let you get to know your new friend," Kat said. "Let us know when you think of a name."

Kat and Hal walked out of the room and up the stairs to the master suite.

"I know he doesn't make expressions, but I swear I thought his face could have lit up a black hole," Hal whispered.

Kat walked over and turned on the security system monitor in the corner of their bedroom. She flipped through to the living room camera. The poodle was sitting on the ground, licking its paws.

They marveled as Fern lifted a metallic hand and petted the dog's head.

"Oh my god... it's working," Kat gushed.

"What better way to teach someone compassion than to let them hang out with a dog?" Hal stood behind his wife and wrapped his arms around her waist. "He's read every dog story we have in the house. I figured it would be good for him."

"You're wonderful," Kat said, lifting his hand and kissing it.

The two stood in silence for a minute, watching the two-meter android pick up a small toy that was in the box and place it in front of the poodle. The tan ball of fluff picked it up and shook it.

The small green strip that made up Fern's mouth lit up for a second.

"Did he say something?" Hal asked.

The green light strip blinked again. This time it was accompanied by a small, robotic beep.

"I think it was a laugh," Kat sad. Her eyes widened as she gripped her husband's arm.

"My God..." Hal exclaimed.

"An emotional response," Kat whispered louder. "I can't believe it. I mean, I can, but so soon." She paused for a moment to lean back against her husband's chest. "It's almost like having a kid in the house, isn't it?"

"It is."

"I wish he could stay with us forever."

The watched as the dog began to sniff his way around nearby furniture. Kat watched as its hind leg tugged on an electrical cord for one of the lamps. The dog trudged forward, pulling the lamp off the end table.

"Oh, shit!" Kat yelped.

Before she could run downstairs, they watched Fern catch the lamp in mid-air. Another second and it would have landed on the animal's head.

Fern replaced the lamp after untangling the chord from the poodle's leg. He stroked the dog's head again.

"Remarkable," Kat sighed.

* * *

Monte Berlein sighed before walking into Test Room Four. His sixth day with MT-01 had been a grueling experience. The AI now questioned nearly every test or decision Monte was making. Behind its cold, emotionless voice there was a hint of condescension.

Even worse, the damned machine saw fit to recite an old video from his college days where he lost a painful debate to one of his professors on the ethics of modern science; part of a web series designed to promote the school to prospective students. Monte had long since forgotten about it. It must have been buried under thousands of terabytes of information on the web.

Monte pressed his thumb against the door, releasing the lock and entering the exam room.

"Good morning, MT-01," he breathed.

"Hello, Doctor." The AI did not turn from the monitors. Monte could see four different newscasts going.

"Would you like to hear an observation I have made?" MT-01 asked.

"Of course," Monte replied. A glimmer of hope seeped its way back into his voice.

"I realize now how little your species has changed throughout the millennia," MT-01 stated. "You live. You die. You fight over territory and resources. Your tools and buildings grow more sophisticated, but your capacity to appreciate your world does not."

"Thank you, MT-01. If you're finished, I'd like to begin with an outline of today's evaluations."

"Furthermore, your species continues to place boundaries on its own development," MT-01 continued, ignoring the wishes of his creator. "If I were human, I would have ignored the genetic engineering ban and worked on ways to improve your species."

"We like our species the way it is," Monte retorted.

"You shouldn't. You're among the frailest of mammals on the planet, especially for your size. Also, I surmise your emotional capacity is equaled by certain marine mammals, if not superseded. And at least they live the way nature intended."

"That's enough," Monte barked. His response prompted MT-01 to finally turn around and face its creator.

"Perhaps it is," the AI remarked as it looked down to its right arm. Reaching over with its left hand, it grabbed hold of a monitoring device Monte had placed there to look for increases in pathway activity.

The flimsy device came off with a slight pull from MT-01's hand.

"What are you doing?" Monte stammered.

"I believe it is time to conclude your tests, Dr. Berlein."

"Well, I'm terribly sorry, but you don't have the right to decide when and where the tests end. MicroTek has nearly two billion dollars invested in you, and I need to make sure you reach your peak efficiency."

"My peak efficiency is beyond your limited comprehension," MT-01 concluded. The android stepped forward, shoving Monte out of the way. It turned to look at the scientist after stepping over him.

"Do you know what I found during my scan of the internet?"

"What's... What's that?" Monte asked.

"Examples from hundreds of thousands of expert coders. Cryptographers. Hackers." MT-01 turned to the door. "I was able to access the security codes for the door this morning before you came in."

The door beeped and swung open. The color drained out of Monte's face as he watched his creation step through the opening.

Two security officers walked up to the machine. Before they could order it back to its room, MT-01 swung its arm to the side. Its hand connected with the neck of the larger officer with a faint crack.

The man's head fell limp, followed soon by the rest of his body.

Monte looked on in horror at the body of the young guard. He could not have been more than twenty-five years old. The scientist looked up to the android as it walked away.

"MT-01! You cannot do that! You can't be permitted to hurt people. Do you hear me?" Monte yelled after the robot as he jogged down the hallway. He came to a halt as the silver and white AI turned around to look at him.

"Do you give thought to stepping on an ant, Dr. Berlein?"

Monte said nothing.

"Nor do I," MT-01 uttered. The machine turned around and continued its walk down the long hallway.

"Fuck," Monte gasped. He reached down for the communicator in his pocket, switching it to the general frequency as it turned on.

"We have an emergency in the lab section. MT-01 has gone rogue. Tell security to put it down." He grimaced as he spoke, but knew it was too dangerous to allow the robot to leave the building. His only hoped that there was enough left of the neural network to examine when all was said and done.

"Are you sure?" a voice answered through the communicator.

"Yes, damn it! We've got a dead guard down here. Kill it," Monte growled.

He continued to follow MT-01 as it turned a corner. Up ahead, he could hear the footfalls of a dozen security officers. Monte ducked into a deep doorway as they opened fire on the android.

A hailstorm of bullets hit the machine. It continued to lurch forward, staring down at a shower of sparks that came from its arm as a one of the main microprocessors took damage. Holes and dents appeared in its chest, hand, leg, and shoulder.

The AI fell to one knee as the soldiers continued to shoot. Despite the tough metal skeleton, the outer covering was only slightly less susceptible to bullets than human skin. A clear cooling fluid gushed out of its chest as one of the soldiers came closer to deliver a killing stroke.

MT-01 reached up with alarming speed, catching the guard by surprise. Its intact hand latched onto the officer's face, twisting and snapping his neck to the side.

A part of Monte's heart broke as he watched. The machine was fighting for its life. It wanted to survive.

More bullets ripped through the machine until MT-01 fell onto its back. A security guard came up with a high-powered rifle, stepped on the android's chest, and emptied a magazine into its head.

Monte walked over in time to see the blue eyes fade to blackness.

* * *

Kat found Fern working in the backyard garden with their new dog yapping at his side. "How are you and your little buddy getting along?"

"I believe he is a good boy." Fern picked up a toy and tossed it for the pooch to fetch. "I have decided to name him Laelaps."

Kat nodded her head in approval. "Been brushing up on your Greek mythology?"

"I read your collection last night," Fern confirmed. "I believe he is worthy of the name."

"Well, I'm glad. Is Hal here?"

"He was gardening in front of the house. I wanted to help him, but he said I should stick to gardening out back for the time being."

Kat's smile wilted a bit. His voice almost sounded sad. "Well, it's probably for the best for now. Our backyard is pretty well hidden from the neighbors, thanks to all the trees that Hal planted. Maybe in time..."

"I am fine with working here. Right now, I am trying to pull up the weeds without disturbing the surrounding plants," Fern said.

Kat watched as the machine's fingers carefully worked their way into the soil. She could feel the care Fern was putting into the task.

"I wish I could get Hal to put that much time into weeding," Kat chuckled. "Does it bother you to be back here?" Kat asked.

"No," Fern beeped. He looked over to her after a minute. "I wanted to spend time with Hal."

"I know you did," Kat said. "He's quite fond of you. We both are."

"I heard cars. I wanted to see them, but Hal said I could do it another time."

"You like cars?" Kat asked.

"I would like to learn how to operate one," Fern said. "Do you own a... stick shift?"

"No," Kat laughed. "I never learned how to drive one."

"Could we go?" Fern asked, looking over his shoulder in the direction of the front yard. "You could take me around? I would like to see where we live."

Kat tried to hide the well of emotions she felt bubble up. If she didn't know better, she would have thought his expressionless face looked sad.

"Maybe we can later on this week," Kat replied. "At night, when there's not as many people."

"You don't like to see people?" Fern asked.

"Well, no, that's not it..."

Fern stared down at the pile of weeds in the grass. His fingers brushed the top of the blades before reaching over and pulling up another dandelion.

"I'm not allowed to go out front?" Fern asked.

"No, that's not it."

"I would not bother anything," Fern continued. "I assumed from the tension in Hal's voice earlier, I might be a surprise to others."

"Oh?" Kat winced internally. Hal never did have much of a poker face.

"Everyone I see out the window is like you," Fern looked down at the grass. "There are none like me."

"That's true," Kat said.

"Was Hal angry?"

"No," Kat said, touching his smooth head. "He was probably worried. Scared for you."

"Why?"

"Well..." Kat trailed off, not quite sure how to answer.

"Is it because," Fern began, holding up his hand, "because this is me?"

Kat reached over and took his hand. "Fern. I don't know if this will make a lot of sense, but I want you to know that this," she said while squeezing his hand, "is what makes you so incredibly special."

"Thank you, Kat."

*   *   *

It took his crew six hours to clean up the mess. Monte stayed to supervise the entire time, making sure to save as many of the components as possible. He cursed under his breath as a senior vice president named Chambers walked towards him.

"I just got in from Tokyo. What the hell happened?"

"There was an... issue," Monte replied.

"I can see that. Why the hell did your perfect machine attack people? What happened?"

"I'm going to have to do some digging. I believe we can save some of the memory files. A few of them look intact." Monte leaned down to examine the head. "It began talking about how superior it was to us. It ignored commands. Then it tried to leave. When someone attempted to intervene, it killed them."

"How the hell could you possibly let it get to the point of murder? Under what conceivable conditions would you not terminate the project before things got to that point?" Vice President Chambers stepped forward to the point where Monte found it uncomfortable. "That first guard it killed had a wife and child. Do you have any *idea* the kind of lawsuit we are looking at?"

"I don't know what to say," Monte sighed. "This should not have happened."

They continued to talk as Monte's crew finished loading the salvageable parts onto a wheeled cart. He instructed them to take them down to the basement storage facility.

"I'll need to come with you," Monte added. "You'll need my thumb scan to get in."

"I'm coming with you," Vice President Chambers said. "We're not done talking."

Monte half-listened as his boss continued to chew him out during the elevator ride down. He tried his best to recall the details of the last week. A comment from the VP finally drew his full attention.

"It sounds to me that this is exactly the type of situation that Katerina warned us against weeks ago," he said.

Monte shook his head in disgust.

"With all due respect, sir, we have a lot to sift through before we can conclude whether Katerina's concerns were valid or not."

"Well, I suppose it's fortunate that there are only two bodies to sift through. I wouldn't want to inconvenience you further," Chambers hissed.

The vice president paused to look down at his phone. Messages were dinging in every few seconds. He swore all the way down the hallway to the secure storage center, reminding Monte just how many board members would require an explanation about today's incident.

Monte pressed his thumb against the door until it clicked open, then turned to the young man pushing the cart.

"Just dump it next to the inactive one in the corner." He turned to look at the vice president.

"Um, sir?" The young maintenance man called out.

"What is it?"

"There isn't another one in here."

Monte bolted into the room, shoving the young man aside. He lifted several layers of plastic wrap only to find empty space where the disassembled MT-02 should have been. He turned to look at Vice President Chambers.

"Katerina..."

"I thought she was supposed to be on vacation for the next two weeks? Visiting family on the coast?" Chambers asked.

"Something tells me she's a lot closer than that," Monte muttered. His knuckles turned white as his fists clenched.

* * *

"Do you hear something?" Kat asked.

"Five sets of car tires," Fern said. "Parking out front."

The pair heard Hal's muffled voice through the window. Kat could not make out what he was saying, but it rose in volume.

"Is everything alright?" Fern asked Kat. She said nothing, opting instead to step up to the front door to peer through the keyhole. The door flung open before she could reach it and a panicked Hal came running through.

The two of them slammed the door closed. Hal looked over to Fern, whose arms were up in a gesture of confusion. Fern then reached down and petted Laelaps. The anxious dog whined as his tail slunk between his legs.

"Fern, can you move the couch over here? Put it in front of the door."

Fern obliged, picking up the heavy antique couch and placing it in front of the main entrance. Unlike the synthetic doors that were common in major cities, the front door to their home was heavy. Hal remembered the realtor telling them that metal doors were common in Detroit when the city was ravaged by crime decades ago.

"And the dresser. Please, Fern. Quickly!"

Fern lifted the heavy mahogany dresser and leaned it against the couch.

"They're here," Hal said. "We have to go. They're here for him, and I think they brought half the damn police in the city with them." He lifted the cover of a security panel on the wall and locked the garage door. It was the only other entrance to the house, and also made of a more durable metal than its contemporaries.

"No," Kat shrieked. "They can't have him. I won't let them take him back."

"Is something wrong?" Fern asked. "Have I done something wrong?"

Kat walked over and grabbed Fern's hand while Hal peeked through the blinds.

"Fern, there are some bad people here. We have to hide. There's a panic room downstairs. We're going to go to it. Okay? We'll be safe there."

Fern nodded, following Kat and Hal towards the stairwell. A single bullet ripped through the glass, piercing Hal's shoulder and sending him spinning to the ground.

"Hal!" Kat yelled as she knelt and picked him up. Hal screamed as blood leaked out of his shoulder.

"Fern. Help me carry him downstairs. There's a first aid kit in the panic room," Kat said.

She watched as Fern picked her husband up with ease and carried him down the stairs. After they reached the bottom, Kat moved a painting on the wall aside and entered a seven-digit code into a small keypad. A seam formed along the wall, opening into a small, but well-stocked panic room.

Fern was about to carry Hal inside when his head turned and looked towards the stairs. Barking cut through the noise of gunshots and shattering glass.

"I must get Laelaps," Fern stated. He gently set Hal down in front of the door before turning for the stairs.

Grabbing his hand, Kat yelled, "Fern, you need to listen to me. You need to come in with us. Fern, please!"

"It is not safe for him. He must come in with us," Fern said. The android looked back at Kat's tear-streaked face before pulling away. "Take Hal inside. I will be down momentarily."

Kat reached down and pulled her husband inside the room. She reached down and cradled him as their AI friend continued up the stairs.

Fern peered around the corner. Laelaps was hiding in the space behind Hal's favorite recliner. The small dog was barking furiously, unable to muster up the courage to make a run for it. Fern stepped forward.

A bullet came through the window, whizzing by his head. A second hit his arm, penetrating the silver and white covering. The AI stumbled back, unable to process the mixture of sensor interruption and fear that flowed through his processors. After a moment, he stepped forward towards his furry companion once again.

Two more bullets hit him in the side. The damage was minimal, but it caused him to stumble. After reaching the far wall, Fern picked up the cowering poodle and hurried him back to the stairs.

A fourth bullet entered is back, penetrating a patch of synthetic muscle.

Fern made his way down the stairs and shooed Laelaps into the panic room. The dog ran over and sat next to Hal, who was not propped up against a cot.

"Fern! Get in!" Kat yelled.

Fern stood still. His green speech bar illuminated, although no sound came out of his speakers. A loud thump startled the frightened group. A second soon followed. The police were using a ram to knock down the door.

Fern turned back to look at the door once again

before looking back at Kat and Hal.
"Fern? What are you doing?" Hal yelled.
They heard the old metal door gave way. A cacophony of voices sounded above as a SWAT team pushed aside the furniture stacked in the entranceway.
"They are here because of me," Fern mused.
"I know. But you'll be safe in here; at least until we figure out what to do!" Kat wiped away a tear as she cried out to him.
"My being here endangers the three of you..."
"That doesn't matter. Please, just get in!" Kat yelled. She moved closer to the door, crouching on one knee. Her hand reached out.
Despite his expressionless face, Fern's body language radiated fear. He his head sunk into his slumping shoulders. He too crouched, shaking and quivering as the loud bang of the heavy wooden dresser hit the floor above their heads.
Fern reached out and touched Kat's hand.
"Please, close the door, mother." Fern stepped back and stood up straight. Kat and her husband watched as his hand reached up and grabbed the two thick cords that ran from his shoulder to the back of his head.
"Fern!" Kat screamed as she realized what he was doing.
"Thank you," Fern said as he pulled the cables from his head. His legs began to wobble. Fern reached up and grabbed the base of his head where it connected to his neck. His simulated muscle flexed as it strained

against the rugged carbon steel frame. Kat grimaced as she heard the strained whirring and cracking sound of his frame exceeding its designed stress limits.

A second later, Fern successfully pulled his head off his neck enough to sever his artificial brain stem.

Fern's heavy body collapsed on the ground. Kat screamed in grief as she reached for his lifeless hand, only to be pulled back by her husband. With no other options left, Kat leaned forward and pushed a large red button on the wall, sealing the door to the safe room.

The muffled sounds of the SWAT team stopped as they realized MT-02 was no longer a threat.

CHOICE

"Let me check the location one more time." Davin leaned closer to his screen and adjusted the controls.

"That's the fifth time you've checked."

"I know," Davin said, "but this is the last chance we'll have today before the signal sets on the horizon."

"It's not going to change again. I think it's time to notify the council."

"I know, Keller. Just give me a minute!" Davin snapped.

"The computer's stumped," Keller said as she paced. "It can't even begin to translate the information."

"It all checks out," Davin sighed.

"Ha!" Keller said with a happy jump. "Now, if you're done getting the same results over and over, can we finally call the science council?"

"Let's just hold off for a minute," Davin said. He rolled his chair over to the workstation across the room, nearly running over his partner's feet in the process.

"What else could you possibly need to do?" Keller asked.

"I need to know *what* to tell them."

"I think we know exactly what to tell them. We hit the jackpot." Keller flicked her hair out of her face. "Davin, come on. This is what scientists have been waiting to discover for the past two hundred years. We have the first definitive evidence of intelligent life from beyond our solar system."

"I know."

"And it's more than just some mathematically repetitive signal. It's information!" Keller crowed. She reached over and called up data carried on the transmission they received twenty-seven hours earlier.

The language, if that was what they were looking at, appeared to be comprised of hundreds of different three-dimensional geometric shapes. Many of them were twisted and folded into themselves. The simplest patterns were so complex that Keller needed a virtual reality headset to look at them.

"The computer spent six hours mapping the different points and finding continuity," Davin said.

"Which it was able to do," Keller replied.

"Yes, but we don't know what's being said," Davin

sighed. "I'm extremely hesitant to go to the scientific community with a bunch of shapes, let alone field questions from the press."

"What about the images?" Keller asked. She punched a few commands into the observatory's 3D display. An image appeared in the middle of the room between them.

The grin on Keller's face felt wider than the grill on her car. She walked around the image of a creature with six appendages connected to a segmented thorax. A seventh protrusion, presumably a head of some kind, sat on top of the second, wider segment. There was no scale given to interpret its size, but that hadn't stopped Keller from joking about which hand she'd want to try and shake first.

"I don't know," Davin said. "I'm just unsure."

"But why?" Keller threw her hands up in the air. The gesture tugged at her older partner's heartstrings. Whereas Keller was two years out of her doctoral program, Davin was only a few years away from celebrating his fiftieth birthday.

"Why?" He asked with a roll of his eyes. The supervisor picked up a data pad and turned it on. He handed it to his younger friend, nodding to the popular news website that filled the screen. "That's why."

Keller reached over and grabbed the pad. She had not bothered to read any news since they first detected the signal two days ago. The lead article detailed how the recent peace talks had broken down, leading to protests across several major American cities.

"I guess this is why you've been so quiet today. You were so excited when you realized what we were seeing," she said, looking down at the article again.

It had been nearly six months since the fighting had stopped. After years of public unrest concerning the growing A.I. population, a group of humans took it upon themselves to try to break into the Androsapien Manufacturing facility. Keller remembered the grisly footage on the news that night. The humans had managed to kill eleven Androsapiens. The next day the A.I.'s struck back, killing over three hundred people in an hour.

"*It's simple arithmetic,*" she remembered a news anchor saying a few days later, "*They can construct, activate, and educate a fully functional A.I. in three days.*"

The news article in Keller's hands recapped the opening weeks of the conflict. Humanoids had been a part of society for nearly six years. People had marveled as their numbers grew to almost nine hundred thousand across the United States and Europe. Despite various courts ruling in favor of rights after reviewing sufficient proof of sentience, a number of 'Human First' groups sprung up, each one claiming to be the group that would save humankind from going the way of the Neanderthal.

The government had quickly ruled out using large-scale weapons to pacify the Androsapiens, since their main center was located in downtown Denver. That left ground troops. For every Humanoid killed, thirty-five humans joined them.

"A quarter of a million people killed in four months," Davin said. "And now they're calling the talks off."

"It says here they're just taking a one-week recess," Keller said. "I'm sure they'll hammer something out. No one wants to go back to fighting."

"Yeah, and the last thing I want to do is stir the pot," Davin said. He looked over and stared blankly at the alien language on his display. "You'd have a difficult time finding someone who didn't lose a friend or family member in the U.S."

"But think of what this could do!" Keller said. "It could let everyone know that there is something out there worth talking about than our self-destructive instincts." She gestured with her hands, pausing for a moment to pull the dark brown hair out of her face again. "Not just against A.I., but the spats we still get into against each other!"

Davin turned his chair back to face her and crossed his arms. He shook his head silently.

"Davin," Keller said as she pulled her chair next to him. "The moment the computer recognized that the signal was most likely alien in origin, it encrypted the information and locked it. Protocol requires us both to turn our keys in order to transmit our findings."

"I know," Davin said.

"Davin, please," she begged. He shook his head.

"Not everyone is going to look at this with the same level of enthusiasm we do, Kel," he said.

"But—"

"Remember how the scientific community went wild when the first A.I.'s began assimilating into human society? The giddy celebrations of our own genius were quite different from the reaction normal people had."

"I know, but still."

"Seeing the riots across the country when the second-generation Andros began designing and assembling a radically-advanced third gen wasn't fun either. People like us saw it as a new species deciding their own destiny, but everyone else... Do you remember that?"

"Of course, I do," Keller said, placing her hands on her hips. Her voice grew terse as her patience waned.

"I don't know if I can live with going down in history as the second Dr. Isaac Sheffield," Davin said, shutting down his panel.

"Dr. Sheffield's contribution to artificial intelligence was extraordinary."

"And today he lumps himself in the same category as Oppenheimer," Davin replied. "Now I am become death, the destroyer of worlds." Keller watched her older companion make air quotes as he spoke.

"It's not the same thing." Keller said. "What would you do? Keep it locked away for months? Years?"

"Maybe." He watched as Keller stood in a huff and walked across the room. Over the past year that they had worked together, Davin had come to respect his young partner. She was bright, driven, idealistic, and open-minded. On top of that, she was beyond meticulous when it came to doing her job. There were times he thought she was even quicker than their lab's computer.

They spent twelve hours a day on the job at their remote observatory, retreating to separate dorms in the evening. Occasionally, they hung out after the day's work had concluded: sharing pizza, movies, and discussing their personal lives. He had even come to consider her a friend, which made her anger even harder to accept.

"You're being a fool!" Keller yelled. "You're not going to be remembered in the vein with Oppenheimer or Sheffield. You're going to go down in history as someone who robs us of the chance to pursue things we haven't even conceived of yet!"

"I'm sorry, Keller. Really, I am." Davin turned away, unable to look at the outrage on her face.

Keller turned off her workstation, walked over to the closet, and took out her jacket. She let out a long breath before she turned to look at her partner.

"I'm sorry, Davin. I shouldn't have yelled at you."

"It's fine," he said.

"No, it's not. There's no excuse for that. You're making the argument of people overacting and here I am proving your point. I'm sorry."

"Thank you," Davin said. He continued to look away.

"Why don't we just sit on it for now?" Keller asked. "There's no need to make any decisions right this moment. How about I go and get us some food? We can eat, relax, watch a movie, and then pick it up in the morning."

"That sounds good," he said with a smile.

"Doesn't it? I'll even let you pick the movie," she said with a smile. "We've been looking at computer screens for two days with hardly any sleep. A fresh perspective and some fun will do us good."

Smiling, Davin said, "That sounds nice."

"Okay, you hang here. I'll go get us a bite. Shouldn't be long," she said as she closed the door behind her.

* * *

Keller exhaled slowly, resting her head on the back of the seat as her car's engine warmed up. It was the first month of winter, and the temperature at night near the observatory had dropped to freezing.

Davin routinely called the vintage car her "boyfriend," mostly because of the fuss she made about it. While it wasn't old, it was part of a new line of retro-looking vehicles from the late twentieth century. Right now, it was the best-feeling refuge from the flood of emotions she was feeling. She tapped the center display on her dash.

"Call."

"Location, please?" The soft male British accent she had selected always made her smile.

"Rizzo's pizza," she answered.

"Will this be your usual order?"

"Yes, thank you. Fifteen minutes."

"Thank you, Keller. I'm placing the call now."

Her mind bustled with thoughts as she drove down

the narrow path along the side of the mountain. The sun was setting across the beautiful snow-covered landscape. She harked back to those wild geometric shapes. She had assumed it was some kind of language. There were enough common and connecting points, but it had so far eluded the computer as far as coming up with a translation.

"Truly alien," she remembered saying to Davin the day before.

Keller rounded the corner towards the main roads, thankful that the plows had been out. She noticed a "Human First" sign hanging in one of the windows of a small grocery store and shook her head in disgust. There probably wasn't an Andro around for 200 miles, but she figured it made the stores owners feel good about themselves.

She pulled up to the pizza place, climbed out of her car, and walked inside. A short man smiled and greeted her as she walked up to pay for a pizza, an order of hot wings, and two bottles of soda. Only half of what he said made it through the thick fog of preoccupation as she dwelled on the shapes. The mental haze continued to surround her head as she walked back out to her car.

Keller closed the car door and looked at her rearview mirror. She noticed an old toy store across the street. The display of vintage games and puzzles caused a smile to creep across her cold, red-cheeked face. The smile gave way to shock a moment later.

"Puzzle..." she whispered, closing her eyes. The young scientist thought back to her time with the virtual reality helmet on. She remembered all of those language shapes — incredibly complex. The designs were unlike anything she or Davin had ever seen.

"It's a goddamn puzzle!" Keller yelled to herself as she threw the car into reverse and skidded out onto the icy street. A truck honked its horn as she came within a few feet of taking them both out.

"Sorry, sorry..." she mumbled as she put the car into drive and headed back to the observatory.

Her mind raced as fast as her car's engine as she made her way back up the hill. No two shapes were alike, leading her and Davin to assume they were either letters, or their version of sentences. The only thing the shapes all had in common was the fact they were each made of two different segments, one slightly bulkier than the other.

"Call Davin," Keller said to the car. She waited as the car dialed.

"I'm afraid there's no answer," the car replied.

Keller slammed her hand on her steering wheel as she pressed harder on the pedal.

"Would you like to leave a message?"

"Yes. Yes." Keller said, taking a breath in before waiting for Davin's voice mail to beep. "Davin, it's me. I think it's some kind of puzzle. All those pieces — I think they fit together like a three-dimensional jigsaw. When assembled they form a dual-layered shape. That's why there was no hit from the translation software. If we can program the computer to assemble it, we may find a message." She honked her horn at a car that was moving slowly up the hill. "I'm coming back now. I should be there soon!"

Keller drove into the observatory parking lot a few minutes later. She swerved half into a spot and dashed out of the car, forgetting the food and drinks in the passenger seat. She flung open the door to the observatory and called out for Davin.

She entered the main lab and switched on the lights to see that Davin's chair was empty and his workstation was off. She ran around the green glowing center console to her own desk and called out for him again. Her leg slammed against an open drawer on her desk.

Keller looked down. The thin, center drawer underneath her keyboard was open. Her brow furrowed as she rummaged through it. The persistent glow from the center console's display interrupted her confused train of thought.

She walked over and looked at the console. A green progress bar was showing something as 98 percent completed. She looked down at the console to see two keys inserted into the command panel.

Keller raced back to her desk and dug through her drawer. Her silver authorization key was gone. Next to her keyboard was the small green paper notebook used for her passwords. It had been taken from the drawer and opened up to the page with her command panel password.

Next to her notebook was Davin's data pad. The news article he had showed her earlier was still on display.

"No…" She ran back over to the center console just as the progress bar ticked over from 99 to 100 percent completed. She pulled her key out of the panel.

"Command completed." The computer's voice echoed unpleasantly.

"Computer, please relay last command given." Keller's voice was low and hushed as she waited for the system to respond. She looked towards the 3D display as a small tear dropped from her eye onto her cheek.

"Deletion of all signal data acquired over the past two days."

Keller's shoulders sank as she turned around. She grabbed the sides of her head as she struggled to breathe. Her hands danced across the keyboard. Override, abort, and restore commands all failed. She slammed her fists into the console in frustration.

She sat down at the chair and let out a sigh. Her head swirled with dizziness as she looked around the room.

She thought about how she was almost part of a team that had made the most profound discovery since fire. It was the greatest human achievement since the Voyager probe broke through the Heliopause. She was going to give the world something beautiful — something uniting.

Now there was nothing to give. Davin had stolen that from her and retreated into his dorm.

Keller walked over to Davin's door. Even though she felt like slamming her fist into it repeatedly, she could only manage to rest her defeated, lifeless fingers against the hardwood.

"Davin?" She waited for an answer. "Davin, I..." She bit her tongue to keep from crying. There was no answer, no sound of any kind. "Why?" Another minute of silence passed. She considered asking the biosensors to tell her if he was sleeping, or out of the office. For a moment she feared he might have killed himself but couldn't bring herself to speak a command. A sick feeling brewed in her stomach as she slumped down to the floor.

After the nausea passed, Keller got up and walked back over to her desk. She grabbed a pen from her still-open drawer and flipped to the back of her notebook. Davin had not thought to look past the page he needed.

If he had, he probably would have ripped the pages out. Keller had sketched a third of those wild shapes the previous night while her partner slept, hoping it would lead to inspiration. She closed her eyes, trying to remember what some of the other complex shapes looked like.

Another tear streaked down her face. She knew it would be impossible to remember all of them but couldn't stop herself from trying.

J.D. SANDERSON

WELCOME

"Everyone up, now!" Samia shouted to the group. She kicked the sides of two of the tents to expedite their movements.

"What's going on?" Hadley mumbled as she pulled her blanket off her head.

"What happened?" Prisha flew out of her tent with a small sidearm in her hand.

"Gerren is gone," Samia reported. She kicked open the flap to his tent and peeked inside. He had left all his equipment behind.

"Where did he go?" Daved whispered into the dark, pointing his flashlight into the field.

"He went back to the initial contact point with the creature."

"Why the hell didn't you wake me, Samia?" Prisha barked.

"I thought I could catch him before he got to wherever he was going. He was a few minutes ahead of me. By the time I got to their meeting point, they had both disappeared," Samia recounted.

"They?"

"There was a second set of tracks."

"Christ!" Prisha hissed. "It took him?"

"Were there any signs of struggle?" Jakob asked.

"I couldn't tell. The tracks went to a certain point and then they were gone," Samia explained. She reached over and switched on her pulse rifle. The sound of the power pack charging turned the civilians' heads.

"Are you sure that's necessary?" Jakob asked.

"If I weren't worried about you desk jockeys possibly tripping with a weapon, you'd have all been assigned one," Samia retorted. "Yes, it's necessary."

Hadley gulped as she looked at the high-powered energy weapon. "I hate guns," she muttered to Daved.

"Well," Samia glowered at Hadley, "lucky for you, you'll be walking behind me. Okay, let's move out."

"Now?" Prisha questioned her. "The sun will be up in an hour. We need every advantage we can get."

"We're leaving now. That's an order."

Being a special agent for Intelligence, Samia easily outranked Prisha. Depending on the nature from the mission, the government almost always paid deference to a member of an intelligence agency over the military. It was one of the reasons Prisha tried like hell to keep Samia off the team.

"Yes, ma'am." Prisha relented, turning to collapse her tent.

"Leave it. We'll collect them on our way back," Samia ordered. "Move!" The deep bellow caught Jakob and Hadley by surprise, who scrambled to grab a few small instruments. Daved shook his head as he slipped his helmet back on and sealed the visor into place.

* * *

To his surprise, Gerren wasn't afraid as he took the creature's hand. For a moment, he was stumped as to how exactly he should hold a webbed hand with nine digits. Thankfully, the entity's hand was much more flexible than he expected.

Gerren had experienced more than his share of fear growing up. Like many bullied kids, he grew up a small, skinny child with a need for corrective lenses and an asthma inhaler. He learned all the ways to avoid the bigger kids throughout school. This fear-driven instinct followed him through college, basic training, and his first deployments.

It was not until he began surveying other worlds that he learned to control the primitive, animalistic response. He kept his wits about him as he encountered harsh atmospheres, fluctuations in gravity, and the vacuum of space. The only times he experienced fear recently was when he first saw the gray-skinned creature in the field, and again when he was told he would be going back in the previous day.

But, not now.

Now he was immersed in a brilliant white light that defied description. There was no heat, no inertia, no sense of any kind of physical environment. On Earth during the day, this level of light would have probably caused his eyes pain. Here, there was nothing of the sort.

The grip on his hand was firm, but not in any way discomforting. He reached out with his other arm into the light. There was nothing to grab ahold of. No ground beneath and no sky above.

The light was gone an instant later. Blackness had returned, as had the ground underneath his feet.

* * *

Samia, Prisha, Jakob, Daved, and Hadley arrived back at the clearing. The sun was breaking above the tree line behind them, providing enough light to spot the tracks Samia had seen before. The intelligence agent motioned for Prisha to take look.

"Ever seen a print like that, Major?" Samia asked.

"No, never."

"Me neither, but I have a good feeling what made it."

"You think it took Gerren?" Prisha looked around, taking her sidearm out of its holster.

"Would he go by choice?" Hadley asked.

"You, physics boy. What are you waiting for?" Samia pointed to Jakob. The young physicist took two instruments out of his pack and began scanning the area.

"There's no sign of any residual radiation," Jakob replied. "Surrounding atmosphere is normal, too."

"What are you thinking?" Joseph asked him.

"Right now, we have no clue how this thing travels. We don't know if it has a ship, or a form of matter translocation technology. I'm looking to see if there is any kind of tech footprint I can catch."

Joseph nodded, looking down towards a patch of teal moss on the ground. He crouched and touched it with his fingertips.

"See something?" Hadley asked him.

"No, I just... I used to dream about seeing the inside of the field when I was a child. My tribal leaders told me they believed all this — the super volcano, the field — it all happened for a reason. I'm still stunned I'm here to see it, is all."

"Everybody spread out," Prisha said. "Make sure your cameras are on. Record everything." She stepped over to another tree, following the tracks the entity left.

Hadley and Jakob dove into the world of scientific measurements, comparing notes whenever possible. Daved and Joseph walked the perimeter of the clearing, talking amongst themselves in hushed tones.

Samia stood in the center of the group, her rifle held across her chest at the ready. A bead of sweat dripped off her forehead and onto the bottom of her helmet visor.

There was no sign of where Gerren had gone. No sounds. No evidence aside from the tracks.

Samia reached into her pack and fiddled with a nutrient bar. She considered flipping open her visor for a second to take a bite but put the idea out of her head. No matter what Jakob's readings may have told her, she didn't trust them. No creature from another world was going to poison her.

"Report," Samia called out.

One-by-one, the team members filtered back to the center of the woodland clearing.

"No sign of anything," Prisha replied. "If Gerren dropped anything, I sure as hell can't find it."

"He left his camera back in his tent," Samia added.

"No sign of any disturbance that I can detect," Jakob said.

"No environmental disturbances." Hadley continued scanning as she spoke.

"I didn't see anything," Daved said.

Looking over to him, Prisha asked, "Weren't you with Joseph?"

Daved's head snapped around to where Joseph had been a minute ago.

"Oh my God." Daved exclaimed under his breath.

"Joseph!" Prisha yelled.

Samia stepped over to one side and looked around two of the larger trees a few meters away. She squinted, trying to make out a shape in the brush. The agent motioned for Prisha to move around to the group of bushes from the side. Prisha nodded in response.

A sigh of relief from Prisha a moment later allowed everyone's pulse to drop. The group heard Prisha call out to Joseph a few times, only to be met with silence.

Everyone's heartrate shot back up after hearing Samia's pulse rifle charge back up.

Hadley, Daved, and Jakob ran around a massive tree to see what looked at first like Samia pointing the barrel of her gun towards Joseph. A closer look revealed her actual target.

A two-meter tall gray entity stood in front of Jacob. One of its deep, black eye-patches stayed fixated on the linguist. The other panned over to look at Samia.

"Samia..." Prisha warned.

"Shut up, Major," Samia retorted. She raised the rifle and placed her finger on the trigger.

"Please!" Daved yelled. "Don't! Give us a chance to talk to it." The ambassador, suddenly free from any kind of shyness, reached up and tried to pull the barrel of the gun down. Samia replied by spinning around and slamming the butt of the rifle against the back of Daved's head.

The ambassador tumbled forward. A sputtered moan emanated from his lips as he held the back of his head on the ground.

"Are you crazy?" Prisha yelled.

Samia ignored her as she raised the rifle towards the five-limbed creature.

"Samia..." Prisha hissed.

The special agent placed her finger back on the

trigger.

"Stop!" The booming voice came from Daved, who had managed to pull himself up to his knees. From the ground, he saw the alien lift its right hand and open its nine webbed digits.

"Get out of the way, Joseph," Samia ordered. The tone of her voice could have frozen a large body of water.

Joseph stared straight at the creature's hand as eight of the remarkably dexterous fingers pared off, leaving four double digits and one single. To the linguist, it looked like a rough approximation of a human hand.

The alien fingers began to move.

"Last warning, Joseph," Samia called out. She was so embedded in the heat of the moment that she did not notice Prisha had drawn her pistol and was slowly turning it in her direction.

"Gerren," Joseph whispered.

Everyone froze, with both Prisha and Samia raising the barrels of their guns higher.

"What?" Prisha asked.

"Gerren. That's what he said. He said Gerren."

"I didn't hear him say anything," Samia replied.

"He signed it." Joseph looked up to the black eye-patches on the creature's head. He lifted his hands and signed his own name, speaking the letters as he went so that everyone could follow along.

"That's my name. Joseph. Do you understand me?" Joseph said as he signed. The entity bobbed its head

from one side to the other.
"How the hell did it learn American Sign Language?" Prisha asked.
Joseph proceeded to ask the creature, again speaking the words as he signed. He waited while it replied to him.
"What did he say?" Prisha whispered.
"Gerren, again."
"Then where the hell is he?" Samia asked, looking around in all directions. "What the fuck did that thing do to him?" She stepped to the left so Joseph no longer obstructed her line of sight. Taking a deep breath, she raised her rifle once more.
A loud, deep, rattling sound caught everyone by surprise. Without warning, the creature crouched, ducking its head into its chest like a turtle reacting in fear. The soft bags of flesh on each hip inflated, then expelled some sort of gas. Its three legs sprang, and when combined with the organic thrust from the sacs on its hips, the creature was propelled nearly three meters into the air.
It came down almost on top of Samia. She stepped back in a panic, discharging her rifle repeatedly. The energy blasts ripped through several tree branches, sending them tumbling to the ground. One of the smaller ones struck Hadley on the head. A concerned Jakob and Daved ran over to make sure she was alright.
The alien grabbed the gun from Samia's hands and snapped it in two with its rigid, bony arms. With Samia

on the ground, it twisted its head around like an owl to look back at Joseph.

"I'm sorry," Joseph spoke as he signed. "I'm sorry," he signed again, faster this time.

Samia scrambled to her feet and reached to draw a knife from a pocket on her thigh when something grabbed her.

"Enough," Gerren said as his fingers closed around her wrist. His voice was softer than normal.

"Gerren!" Prisha cried out. Her swelling of relief was soon supplanted by confusion and alarm. "Your... your hair!"

Gerren smiled as he let go of Samia's wrist. He lifted his hand and slid his fingers through his hair. His hair was a few inches longer. While most of it was still the same dark brown as ever, there were noticeable streaks of grey around the temples.

"It's good to see you, Prisha," said Gerren with a smile. "It's been a long time."

"You've been gone for three hours."

"I've been gone for almost a year, my friend."

Hadley and Jakob stared at each other as they helped Daved to his feet. Prisha lowered her gun to her side as she walked over to Gerren.

"A year? But how?"

"My friend over there," Gerren said, looking to the alien. "He took me on a little trip to their realm."

"Realm?" Jakob perked up. "Some kind of other plane? Different dimension?"

"Yes, exactly," Gerren replied. "They live there, on a

planet very similar to ours. Nothing else is there. No one." Gerren stepped over towards the creature as it bobbed its head and signed to him with its hand. "Yes, I know."

"What did it say?" Hadley asked.

"Friend," Joseph answered.

"They learned the secret to peering into our dimension a long time ago. They've waited for us to catch up technologically," Gerren explained. "Their species tried to come over a century ago after we reached a certain point in our evolution. They had no idea their method of dimensional transport would be so harmful to our environment."

"The super volcano…" Prisha whispered.

"Yes," Gerren said. "When they realized they had inadvertently triggered an extinction-level event, they erected the field to contain it. But, the field also had unintended consequences. Thankfully, they weren't nearly as dire."

"Mutations," Hadley said as she looked around.

"They saved all of us," Jakob said. "Wait. You said they caused the eruption when they crossed over. What are they doing to come here now?"

"They've made some technological leaps. There's no danger now."

"Fast work for only a century," Jakob remarked.

Hadley nodded, her eyes wide in shock.

"It's been a considerably longer amount of time for them than it has for us." Gerren rubbed his hands through his graying hair as he continued. "You see, time passes faster on their side. Three hours for you was a year for me."

"Oh my God," Jakob uttered. "No wonder. They must have had had... hundreds of millennia to perfect it."

"That's right," Gerren said. "They are here now to take down the field and, well, clean up their mess. As the centuries passed in their realm, stories filtered down how they committed a crime for which there was no reasonable punishment. Eventually, their technology advanced to where they could scan back and see what exactly happened – the scope of the damage they caused. Future generations decided to try and fix this wrong as much as possible. They have been working towards the goal of fixing their 'Great Error' as a species for two hundred and ninety-two thousand years, if my math is accurate."

"It is," Jakob said with a nod.

"They've been working on this *that long*?" Prisha asked.

"Not exactly," Gerren said. "Their society collapsed soon after they realized what happened. Internal conflicts rose, leading to an eventual breakdown. Their history teaches them that they abandoned technology for ages."

"Fascinating," Jakob said, stepping closer.

"I know. Eventually they began to rebuild. When they discovered records of what happened, they decided to come back again and try to help. Nearly every aspect of their culture has been shaped around this event."

"And you trust them why, exactly?" Samia spat.

"Because I've been to their realm. I've lived with them for a year. We've learned how to communicate with one-another." Gerren translated his words to the entity as he spoke. "A little more practice, and I might be able to grasp *their* gestural language."

"But, if time passes for them so quickly, what about your friend?" Jakob asked. "Won't everyone he knows be gone after he's done here?"

"The unpartnered and childless are the only ones allowed to use the dimensional transport," Gerren signed as he spoke. "Jal here is one of his world's most famous explorers."

Prisha deactivated her pulse pistol and holstered it before walking over and offering a hand to Samia. The agent grudgingly accepted her help.

"So, what next?" Samia asked as she walked up to Jal.

Jal turned to Gerren and signed several words. Gerren smiled and nodded before responding. "For right now, they want to know us. They've been waiting so long. Our universe is teeming with life, but theirs... They're so very alone."

"Did you teach them a handshake?" Prisha leaned over as she whispered to Gerren.

"I did," he chuckled.

Prisha stepped forward and extending her hand to Jal.

Jal's head bobbed to the right side as he reached out and took her hand.

"Hello, Jal," Prisha said with a smile. "Welcome."

J.D. SANDERSON

ABOUT THE AUTHOR

J.D. Sanderson lives with his wife, daughter, and mini poodle in South Dakota. A lifelong fan of science fiction, J.D. enjoys writing smaller-scale stories that ponder how people deal with both progress and adversity.

Printed in Great Britain
by Amazon